"What's your hurry?" drawled an amused voice

"Blade!" she gasped as she ran into him and tried to untangle herself from his arms. Her face flooded with color at being caught trying to slip back into the house unnoticed.

"What's wrong, my dear? Have you seen a ghost?" he said in a bantering tone.

She was pricklingly conscious of his hands still gripping her arms, his fingers acting like electric charges on her bare flesh. It was ridiculous! She'd never reacted this way before with any man. It was the jet lag that was doing it, of course. In her weakened state she'd allowed Blade Ryan to get under her skin.

"You . . . you startled me, that's all, jumping out of the bushes like that." She hoped he hadn't noticed her peculiar reaction. To let him see any weak spots in her armor would be fatal.

Elizabeth Duke says that her main interest and love is writing, although she's awfully fond of traveling, too. She's visited almost every state in her native Australia and has traveled to New Zealand, the U.S., Canada and Mexico, which leaves her with no shortage of fascinating settings for her romance novels. The author is married and has two children.

Books by Elizabeth Duke

HARLEQUIN ROMANCE
2833—SOFTLY FLITS A SHADOW

Windarra Stud

Elizabeth Duke

Harlequin Books

TORONTO • NEW YORK • LONDON
AMSTERDAM • PARIS • SYDNEY • HAMBURG
STOCKHOLM • ATHENS • TOKYO • MILAN

Original hardcover edition published in 1988
by Mills & Boon Limited

ISBN 0-373-17023-8

Harlequin Romance first edition October 1988

CHAPTER ONE

'LADIES and gentlemen, this is your captain speaking. We will be arriving in Sydney shortly. Thunderstorms are expected, with heavy rain and wind squalls . . .'

Kelly grimaced as she tightened her seat-belt. Stormy weather ahead . . . Was that a portent of things to come? A portent of the kind of reception she could expect from the people at Windarra Stud?

One thing was sure, they were hardly likely to rush out and welcome her with open arms! As a stranger to the valley, as an American—a *foreigner*—and above all, as Rowena Shaw's daughter, she was bound to be regarded with suspicion, at least to begin with.

She chewed on her lip. What must the Windarra people be thinking at this moment, knowing that Rowena Shaw's daughter was on her way to their valley? Coming not as a visitor, but as the new owner of Windarra Stud!

With shaky fingers she drew her powder-compact from her cherry leather shoulder-bag. She was still in partial shock over the startling news that had greeted her a week ago on her return from the European show-jumping championships . . . the news that her mother's first husband, Mungo Heath, had died of a sudden heart-attack on his property in New South Wales, Australia, and that he had left everything he possessed—his thoroughbred stud-farm, his home, his horses, his cattle, his car, even a single-engine light plane—to 'the daughter I never knew, Kelly Nagle'.

She recalled how she had swayed at the news, needing the support of the solemn-faced lawyer who had flown all the way from Australia to give her the news in person.

Why should Mungo Heath, her mother's first husband, who had washed his hands of both his first wife and his unborn child nearly twenty-five years ago, leave his entire estate to her—to the daughter he had never known, had never *wanted* to know?

She tried to steady her hands as she raised her compact to inspect her face in its tiny mirror. Shiny nose, worn-off lipstick, lack-lustre hair, shadowed eyes ... She set her mind to the practical task of repairing the damage, resolutely closing her mind to anything else.

A dab or two of powder disposed of the shine on her nose, a few strokes of coral lipstick brightened her lips and at the same time did wonders for her whole face; a flick through with her comb brought back the glossy sheen to her silky black hair, cut in the short simple style she favoured. There wasn't much she could do about the smudgy shadows beneath her blue eyes—eyes that turned a deep shade of violet in certain lights, or as now, when she was tired. It had been a long, wearying flight from Los Angeles to Sydney, and her travels weren't over yet. Windarra Valley, she knew, lay more than a hundred miles to the north of Sydney. A thirty-five-minute flight by air, her mother had told her. Longer, naturally, by road.

She wondered, as she had numerous times already, if anyone from Windarra Stud would be at the airport to meet her, or if she would have to find her own way to Windarra Valley. When she had called from Los Angeles to give her expected hour and date of arrival, Joe McQueen, the gruff-sounding studmaster at Windarra Stud, had told her that he would 'try' to be at the airport to meet her but that it 'might be difficult' to fly down himself as it was the height of the breeding season, their busiest time of year. 'If I can't get away I'll try to get someone to drive down and pick you up,' he had offered grudgingly. She had hastily told him not to put anyone out, and that was how they had left it.

She sighed as she put the comb and compact back into her bag. Joe McQueen and the rest of the staff at Windarra would understandably have reservations about Windarra's new owner ... a *woman* for a start, a woman of barely twenty-four, who despite a remarkably successful show-jumping career was a newcomer to racehorse-breeding and the horse-racing world, who knew absolutely nothing about Australian conditions, and had never even set foot on the property she had inherited from her father—a man she had never even known. And had never missed, having been adopted at birth by her mother's second husband, Chuck Nagle, who had loved and raised her as his own child.

She let her dark head loll back against the seat. Would the people at Windarra be hard to win over? Would they resent her being the daughter of Rowena Shaw, Mungo Heath's runaway wife? Even those who hadn't been there in Rowena's day would have heard the story of the beautiful American movie star who had surprised the world by giving up a promising Hollywood career to marry an unknown Australian racehorse-breeder called Mungo Heath and burying herself, as Rowena herself liked to put it, in the backblocks of New South Wales . . . only to run away three years later—shocking the world further—after tumbling head over heels in love with a visiting American film producer called Chuck Nagle. Rowena had married Chuck Nagle only weeks before her daughter was born. Mungo Heath's daughter . . . Rowena had been three months pregnant when she met and fell in love with Chuck Nagle.

Kelly swallowed. She had been eight years old when her mother told her the truth—that Chuck Nagle was not her real father, that he had adopted her at birth, and that her natural father was Rowena's first husband Mungo Heath, who had relinquished all rights to Kelly before she was born. Rowena had assured Kelly that Chuck loved her as if she were his own flesh and blood—more so, since he was unable to have children of his own—while her real father had cut her out of his life before she was born, saying he never wanted to see his child, or hear from his wife again.

Kelly recalled the way Rowena's voice had turned bitter as she spoke. 'As far as Mungo was concerned, both of us were dead—out of his life for ever.' Tossing her dark curls, she had hastened to add, 'Anyway, darling, it was for the best. I wanted you to grow up in a stable, loving family unit without any tug-of-war between Chuck here in Los Angeles and your real father half-way across the world. I wanted your happiness above everything, dear. *I* was the child of divorced parents—a cruel, bitter divorce. I wouldn't have wanted you to suffer the kind of life I had to—torn between two fathers, a real father and a stepfather, never knowing where I really belonged or if either loved me for myself or merely wanted me around to spite the other.'

As the backthrust of the aircraft's engines shook the seat beneath her, Kelly tensed. Not so much in fear of the plane's landing as at the uncertainty of what lay ahead. She shook her head ruefully. Most likely Joe McQueen and the rest of the staff at Windarra Stud were hoping she wouldn't stay long . . . that she would take one look at her inheritance and decide to sell up and scuttle back to Los Angeles, as her mother had done before her . . .

She was unprepared for what lay in wait for her in the terminal building. As she emerged from Customs, pushing her trolley of suitcases ahead of her, a barrage of cameras and pen-wielding journalists pressed around her.

'Miss Nagle, are you planning to settle in Australia for good?'

'Does this mean you're giving up your show-jumping career?'

'Is it true that you were thinking of retiring in any case, now that your favourite show-jumper Pixie has died?'

Kelly winced at the reference to Pixie, who had caught a virus only weeks before the European tour, and died days later. The tour hadn't been the same without her. She nodded faintly, looking around helplessly, her head reeling. She hadn't anticipated this . . . not all the way out here in Australia.

'What does your mother Rowena Shaw think of your inheriting Mungo Heath's estate?'

'Did you know Chuck Nagle wasn't your real father?'

'Were you shocked to learn . . .'

With a strangled gasp, Kelly tried to shut out their voices, to hide her face from their cameras. At the same moment, she felt a firm hand grasp her arm, and before she could shake it off with an indignant, 'Let go!' a deep voice rumbled in her ear, 'I've a cab waiting. Come with me!' and she felt herself being swept away, her rescuer's free hand taking charge of the trolley, while the strong fingers of his other still gripped her arm.

'No questions!' the man barked at the pursuing press. 'Can't you see Miss Nagle is exhausted? She's just flown in from Los Angeles. No interviews! And no, she's not posing for any damned pictures either!'

Could this be Joe McQueen, Mungo Heath's long-time studmaster? Kelly wondered dimly as she was bundled away. Surely not? The man was too young . . . mid-thirties at the most, whereas Joe McQueen, from what her mother had told her, would have to be in his late fifties by now. Their voices were different too, it occurred to her now. Joe's over the phone had had a gravelly roughness, a marked Australian twang. This man's voice was more polished; an educated voice, rich and deep and resonant, with authority and confidence to spare. And something else . . . something that overrode the irritation he justifiably felt. Contempt? If that were so, she had the uneasy feeling it was directed as much at her as at the preying journalists.

She eyed him furtively. Whoever he was, he was obviously accustomed to giving orders—and being obeyed. He was fit and tanned and looked immensely strong. *Who was he, and where was he taking her?*

She watched warily as he approached the taxi he had waiting and handed her bags to the driver.

'After you,' he said, swinging open the rear door.

She didn't move. 'I'm grateful to you for getting me out of there, but would you mind telling me who you are and where you're taking me?' she demanded.

'Oh, hell.' The man didn't smile; his irritation was still apparent. 'Didn't Joe McQueen tell you he wouldn't be able to come and meet you himself?'

'You're from Windarra?' she asked, her qualms subsiding.

'Look, mind if I answer your questions on our way into the city? We'll have the Press on our heels if we don't move.' She noticed he was tapping his foot.

She frowned faintly. Why the city? And why in a *taxi*?

Joe had said he'd send a car for her if he was unable to fly down himself. If Joe hadn't come, where was the car?

She looked up at him with the questions trembling on her lips, but he forestalled them with a sardonic, 'I assure you I have no intention of running off with you,' which brought a swift flush to her cheeks, part embarrassment, part defiance. She deliberately gave him one of her 'cool' looks, heavy with scorn.

'You'd regret it if you did,' she said spiritedly, and missed his reaction, if any, as she ducked her head to climb into the car.

'George Street,' the man rapped at the driver before sliding into the seat beside her. He had to bend quite a bit to achieve this, his massive shoulders and long legs taking up so much room in the back seat that she found herself edging closer to the door on her side.

She turned to face him, waiting for the answers he had promised her. He was wearing blue-tinted sunglasses which made it difficult to meet his eyes directly. She concentrated her gaze instead on his mouth. The same derision she had heard in his voice was in the curl of his lips, but under her scrutiny it dissolved into *almost* but not quite a smile.

'I really am grateful to you for rescuing me back there,' she repeated stiffly, wondering why she felt so wary, so ill at ease with this man. It was unlike her to feel uncomfortable in the company of any man. She had lived and worked for years among men—as their equals.

The mocking smile turned to a sneer. 'But surely you're used to being hounded by photographers? An internationally renowned show-jumper, with an equally famous film-star mother?'

She looked at him sharply. His hostility was openly directed at her now rather than at the cameras. If he resented her coming, why had he put himself out to come and meet her?

'On the contrary, I prefer to keep a low profile,' she answered coldly.

His brow shot up. 'You do? You mean having your photograph splashed over the front cover of an international fashion magazine, with a double-page spread inside giving details of your glamorous life and equally glamorous connections, is keeping a low profile?' His lip curled. 'My mother pointed the article out to me—she finds it amusing to keep up with what's going on in the world of the rich and the famous,' he drawled, cool insolence lacing each word.

That damned interview! Kelly thought bitterly. The only one she had ever agreed to do, despite the hundreds of requests for interviews and photographic spreads she had had over the years. She had finally agreed to do just one interview, for a magazine she had always considered in good taste; not for the publicity—she had asked her interviewer specifically not to mention her mother, or to over-glamorise her show-jumping career, a request which had been ignored—but simply because she had needed the money at the time—and the money *had* been good. Show-jumping was an expensive career, with a lot of travelling involved, and her prize-money didn't always cover the exorbitant costs incurred. Rowena and Chuck had helped her in the early days, but she had long since insisted on standing on her own two feet.

She opened her mouth to flash back a sharp retort about a girl needing to take on extra jobs occasionally to support a career like show-jumping, but she managed to restrain herself. She had a feeling the man was baiting her deliberately.

'I don't think I caught your name?' she said icily.

'A thousand apologies, Miss Nagle. Or may I call you Kelly? My manners are a bit rusty these days, I'm afraid. My friends tell me I spend far too much time in the bush.'

There was absolutely nothing of the backwoods bushman about this polished, supercilious stranger, but she let it go, waiting with exaggerated patience for him to introduce himself. For some reason he was trying to push her off-balance, possibly even to make her lose her temper. *Why?* So that she would burst out with what she really thought of him, and of Australia, and of her reception so far?

Why would that matter to him?

'Blade Ryan,' he said at length, with cold politeness, his

hand shooting out to swallow her own. 'You may have heard of the Ryans of Bilba Stud. Your nearest neighbours.'

She nodded, her eyes flicking wider, interested despite herself. She was very conscious of his hand enveloping hers, reluctantly noting its firmness, its strength. And its warmth—incongruously at odds with the coldness of his tone. 'Yes, I have. How do you do, Blade?' she murmured with a cool politeness to match his. Underneath she did not feel so calm. Why did she feel so on edge with this man? He was only a neighbour; nobody to be nervous about!

He still hadn't released her hand, she realised, and she didn't want to draw attention to it by attempting to pull free.

Why had a *neighbour* come to pick her up instead of Joe McQueen or somebody else from Windarra Stud?

'You're—er—taking me into the city to meet someone from Windarra?' she hazarded, looking at him inquiringly—and frowning when she saw only her own image reflected in the tinted lenses. She let her eyes drop to his lips. They were well shaped lips, with something about them—a sensuality combined with firmness, that made her wonder idly what it would be like to trace the outline of that broad, sensual mouth with her fingertips . . .

Shocked at her wayward reaction to a complete stranger—a decidedly arrogant, unlikeable stranger at that!—she let her eyes swerve away to the relative safety of a deeply tanned cheekbone.

As if he had read her frown—she hoped that was all he had read!—he reached up with his free hand and lazily removed the obstructing sunglasses. Involuntarily she flinched under the impact of metallic grey eyes fringed by lashes as thick and dark as her own.

She swallowed, catching her breath slightly as the pressure of his hand on hers increased. A small, mocking smile played around his lips as he lowered his gaze to examine the hand he held captive.

'My, your hand is so small, so slender . . . and so soft. How do you manage to control those powerful show-jumpers you ride, a slip of a thing like you?'

She glared at him, irritated by his tone as much as his words. Patronising devil!

'I'm surprisingly strong—far stronger than I look,' she retorted in her most steely tone, and as if to demonstrate her strength she made another, successful attempt this time, to free her hand. It was an empty victory, as he released it without resistance.

She swung her head away. It seemed safer to look out of the window, even though all she could see below the low blanket of ominously dark cloud were darting cars and trucks and an occasional lumbering bus, with glimpses through the heavy traffic of unremarkable buildings and shop-fronts.

'Racehorses are difficult to handle too . . . even more so,' she heard Blade Ryan murmur, disconcertingly close to her ear. 'Thoroughbred-breeding is not for the faint-hearted. Handling stallions is no mean feat for even the strongest man.' There was a subtle emphasis on the word *man*. 'But perhaps you have already had experience in that area?' he asked smoothly.

She flushed angrily. Now she had an inkling of what he had been leading up to. And perhaps why he appeared to resent her . . .

'I have had no experience in breeding racehorses, no,' she admitted levelly. 'But I have *trained* thoroughbreds—many times. My parents gave me an ex-racehorse for my eighteenth birthday.' She took a deep breath. 'My mare, Pixie . . . I trained her myself and we had many successes together until . . .' She gulped as emotion swelled in her throat. She didn't want to talk about Pixie to this unfeeling stranger. 'I've trained other thoroughbreds—ex-racehorses among them—as well,' she added tightly. 'We tend to use thoroughbreds in show-jumping rather a lot in the States. And you haven't answered my question,' she reminded him sharply.

'Question? Oh, about whether we're meeting someone. Sorry. I was . . . diverted.' His gaze flicked downwards, resting deliberately on the hand in her lap, the hand she had snatched away from his, and she had consciously to fight down the warmth that threatened to sweep up her throat into her cheeks—even though she felt more insulted than complimented by his bold, derisive scrutiny. 'No,' he said easily. 'I'll be flying you back to Windarra myself. Joe and his boys are flat out at present. It's the height of the breeding and foaling season out here. I had to fly down to Sydney yesterday on business, so I said I'd stay overnight and bring you back with me this morning. But I'm afraid I didn't allow for the weather. Apparently Sydney's about to be hit by a storm. We won't be able to fly out until it clears. When I saw those cameramen waiting for you I thought the best thing to do would be to bring you into the city, where we can escape them by hiding in my apartment.'

'Y-your apartment?' Really, this was ridiculous. She was as jumpy as a bird. No man had ever made her feel so—so *unnerved* before. Not even Harvey Quinn. Famous, handsome, sought-after Harvey, who of all the girls he could have chased, had chased—and wanted—her.

'The family keeps an apartment in town,' Blade answered. 'I'm down quite often, and my mother and other members of the family use it on occasion too. You can freshen up and change and then I'll take you out to lunch.'

'Thank you.' Despite his peremptory air, she felt herself relaxing slightly. Abrasive as he was, the man was only trying to be kind. Neighbourly. Australians were like that, she had heard. Why couldn't she take him at face value, and not delve into what might or might not be going on under the surface?

'So . . . you're at Bilba Stud,' she said, settling back in her seat. The Ryans, she knew from her mother, lived in the neighbouring Bilba Valley—the two valleys, Bilba and Windarra, being separated only by a narrow spur which ran north from the mountains. In Rowena's time the Ryans had lived there with their two sons and a baby daughter. The boys would be well into their thirties by now, Rowena had calculated, and the girl would be a few months older than Kelly. 'I dare say she's married by now and living elsewhere . . .' *If she has any sense*, her mother might just as well have added.

'Will and Grace Ryan ...' Kelly remembered aloud. 'Your parents?' she asked Blade, and he nodded. 'My mother has mentioned them ...' She nearly said 'often', but decided that wouldn't be strictly accurate. Rowena had said little over the years about her three-year marriage to Mungo Heath, answering Kelly's questions with a reluctance that hadn't encouraged further questioning. After learning of her inheritance—was it really only days ago?—Kelly had insisted on knowing more, but her mother had not been particularly forthcoming, even then.

'It all happened so long ago, darling, and all I remember is the loneliness and the boredom. My marriage to Mungo Heath was a ghastly mistake. Oh, I was in love with him when I married him. I must have been, mustn't I, to want to give up a successful Hollywood career to go and bury myself in a valley full of horses and cows? Mungo loved me too, in his way, but he was *married* to his precious bloodstock. He expected me to feel the same. I tried, heaven knows, for three long years, but I failed dismally. I hated it there. I was bored to tears. The Ryans were our only real friends ... I guess they hate me now. I guess everyone does.'

'I'm sure it's all forgotten,' Kelly had soothed, hoping it was.

'Damn Mungo Heath!' her mother had said stamping her foot. 'We've had no contact in all these years—I thought he'd forgotten us. He's done this to spite *me*. To spite Chuck and me. Claiming you as his daughter *now*, after all these years ... leaving you that dreadful remote place! He's done it to push a wedge between us ... to take you away from us. It's his way of hitting back at *me*!'

Kelly recalled how she had almost laughed aloud at her mother's histrionics. 'Oh Mother, I've been leading an independent life for years. I've been away, either touring or training, more than I've been at home. How could he be taking me away from you? I may not even stay out there ... how will I know until I see the place? There'll never be a wedge between us, Mother—don't be ridiculous. And I'll always love Chuck too.' She had long ago fallen into the habit of calling him Chuck rather than 'Dad'.

'Look,' she admitted to Rowena. 'I'm sorry I never met my—met Mungo Heath; but, Mother, you and Chuck have been wonderful parents. I couldn't have asked for better. You didn't deny me what I wanted most in all the world—to work with horses—even though neither of you really approved. And Mungo Heath knew about my love of horses and my show-jumping successes before he died. He knew I was happy—and that made *him* happy, his lawyer told me.'

Blade Ryan's deep voice intruded on her thoughts, his tone emotionless now, the mockery gone for the moment. 'I'm afraid you won't be able to meet my father. He died four years ago. He was killed in a light-plane crash.'

'I'm sorry.' Kelly's regret was instant and genuine as she turned to face him. 'I didn't know . . . I'm sure my mother doesn't know either. We don't get much news from Australia, I'm afraid, in our part of the world. And of course——' she hesitated '—my mother's been out of touch with Bilba and Windarra for a long time.' Not wanting him to seize on that particular point, she asked quickly, 'And you're now running Bilba yourself?'

He nodded. 'I came back home the moment I heard about my father's accident—and I've been running the place ever since. Over the next four years I came to know Mungo Heath probably better than anyone. He was like a father to me.' There was a hint of anger in his voice, tinged with something else that might have been bitterness. Was he bitter on Mungo's behalf, because his friend had been denied the chance to be a *real* father in his lifetime? Or was he vexed simply because he had lost a close friend, because he was stuck now with a neighbour he didn't want?

'There's a lot of rivalry and petty jealousies in our business,' Blade went on after a pause, 'but it was never that way between Mungo and me, between Windarra and Bilba. We had a healthy respect for each other. If anything, I guess you could call it a friendly rivalry—and we liked each other too. We often consulted one another, and discussed things together.' The high regard he plainly felt for Mungo Heath had injected the first tinge of warmth into his voice.

Kelly found herself looking at him with new eyes. So, he had been a close friend of her father's. She could learn a lot from this man about the father she had never known. But here in a taxi, with a stranger listening, was not the time.

'And your mother?' she asked. Rowena had described Grace Ryan rather wryly as 'the ideal outback wife and mother, a plain woman with a big heart and boundless energy, dedicated to her husband and family, a woman who loved the valley and thrived on hard work, taking setbacks in her stride'. To Grace Ryan, according to Rowena, the Bilba horses and foals were as much her 'family' as her own children had been.

'My mother is well,' Blade Ryan answered, the cynical lines round his mouth easing further. 'She walks with a stick now, which she hates—she suffers from arthritis—but she never complains. She still lives at Bilba, at the family homestead. She's looking forward to meeting you.'

Kelly hid her surprise behind a non-committal smile. He's just being polite, she told herself. Neighbourly. Mouthing platitudes. Though somehow Blade Ryan didn't strike her as a man who said things simply to be polite. If his mother really did want to meet her, did it mean that she nursed no lasting grudge against Rowena for running out on Mungo Heath, the Ryans' good friend, all those years ago? Or against Mungo Heath's daughter for not contacting her father in his lifetime?

She realised Blade Ryan was speaking again, and she shook herself slightly, as though shaking away the phantoms that still haunted her.

'My brother Ambler and his wife and baby son live in Sydney. They have training-stables there.' Blade leaned towards her as he spoke, and she caught a whiff of his aftershave, which seemed to have a heady portion of his own distinctly masculine odour mixed up with it. 'Our sister Megan, who's about your age, is a nursing sister in a country town not far from Bilba Valley. She's engaged to our stud-groom Dan Cassidy, who lives in a cottage on the property.'

'Your sister wasn't interested in working with horses like her father and brothers?' Kelly asked, maintaining her neutral smile—which wasn't easy, with Blade Ryan sitting so close.

He stroked his chin, drawing her attention to the firm line of his jaw and the deep cleft below the well shaped lips. She looked quickly away, remembering the last time her eyes had dwelt there.

'Our parents always encouraged us to do our own thing,' Blade went on, mercifully unaware, she hoped, of her wayward thoughts. '"There are other things in life than Bilba",' they used to tell us, 'and we've all pursued other careers. Megan chose nursing, following in our mother's footsteps; Ambler studied accounting and business management, and I chose veterinary science—and flying, which has always been a passion of mine. Now Ambler and I are both back in the thoroughbred business, and Megan helps out at Bilba whenever she has any spare time. If I hadn't come back, I guess Ambler would have taken over. Or even Megan, though it's a tough life for a woman on her own.'

Was there a message there? Kelly wondered with wry suspicion.

Blade's eyes didn't so much as flicker as he went on. 'Still, once Megan's married to Dan, they might want to work together as a *team*. Megan's already talking of giving up nursing and maybe taking over the books at Bilba. Mother's getting past it now. She's been doing most of our book-keeping for years, with odd bits of help.'

A vivid flash momentarily brightened the dim interior of the taxi. Kelly, startled, spun her head round. 'What was that?'

'Only lightning. I think we're just going to make it,' said Blade. His last words were drowned by an explosive clap of thunder overhead. Kelly leapt upright in her seat, involuntarily swaying closer to Blade Ryan. She felt his hand on hers, his fingers curiously warm and comforting.

'It's going to come down in buckets. Be ready to jump out.'

It was as though night had fallen suddenly in the middle of the day. The traffic had slowed to a crawl. Headlamps and neon signs were springing on. Pedestrians were scurrying for cover. As their taxi pulled into the kerb below a narrow-fronted old-style apartment building, Blade reached across to fling open her door.

'In you go—*run*! I'll bring the bags.'

Large drops of rain were already spattering the pavement as Kelly dived for cover. A gust of wind caught her hair and blew it in dark strands across her face. Just as she reached the canopied entrance, the heavens opened and with a deafening roar the rain came down in a blinding grey sheet.

She watched, shaking her hair from her eyes, as Blade, barely visible through the torrent of thudding rain, retrieved her bags from the rear of the car. She was holding the door open as he lurched towards the building, a bulky suitcase in either hand, his head bowed, his tawny hair already plastered to his head.

Inside the lobby, he shook himself, and droplets of water flew from his hair. His wet shirt clung to his muscular chest and shoulders like a second skin. He put her two suitcases down and rang for the lift.

'You look as if you're planning to stay for more than the weekend,' Blade commented drily, a faint frown settling between his eyebrows.

She shrugged. 'It's a long way to come just for a weekend,' she murmured evasively. Blade Ryan, it appeared, was another one who didn't expect her to stay! Or *want* her to?

'Yes, of course.' His tone was almost conciliatory, and she glanced at him suspiciously, not sure that the tone rang true. 'I hope you do stay longer,' he said expansively. Water was trickling down his face into his shirt-collar. Minute droplets glistened on the ends of his thick lashes, turning the grey irises below to liquid silver. 'It's natural you'd want to take a good look at the place where your father lived.'

Where you might have lived too—was he thinking?—*if your mother hadn't run off with another man!*

The door slid open and they squeezed into the small lift together, with Blade's long legs straddling the two suitcases. He smelt of dampness and aftershave and a tangy breath-catching masculinity—a heady combination that made Kelly feel curiously light-headed, almost shy—a new experience for her. She was used to mingling with men— from humble grooms to Olympic Gold Medallists, from the lowliest of men to men of the world, the odd prince and president included, and she had never felt uncomfortable in their presence. Why now? What was there about this man that he had this unsettling effect on her?

The Ryan apartment on the fifth floor was compact, modern and functional, furnished in neutral ivory and beige tonings, with splashes of colour in the lampshades and cushions and the few well chosen ornaments. There were two bedrooms, as Blade pointed out, each with an adjoining bathroom, as well as a kitchen and a large L-shaped lounge with a small round table at the kitchen end.

'You'd better get out of those wet clothes,' Kelly said, and at once wished she could snatch the words back. She was only stating the obvious, and the suggestion, once out, sounded cloyingly presumptuous—like something a mother or a wife would say. Swift colour leapt to her cheeks.

Blade mercifully had his back to her. 'You might like to freshen up and change too,' he said, striding into the nearest of the two bedrooms with her suitcases. 'Have a shower. Afterwards I'll take you out to lunch. I've booked a table at the Waterfront. It's a fish restaurant in The Rocks district—one of Sydney's oldest residential areas, which has been largely demolished and rebuilt. It's not far from here.'

Following him, she paused in the doorway, waiting for him to come out again and go to the other bedroom. So . . . she watched him with narrowed eyes. He had booked a table for lunch already, had he? He was very sure of himself—and of her, she thought, unaccustomed to having a man taking control of her life and making decisions without deferring to her first. Let alone giving her orders!

Other men had tried—Harvey Quinn had tried—but she had always managed to hold the upper hand, had always felt that she was in full control of her actions. And now here was this stranger, this neighbour, not even anyone to do with Windarra Stud, organising her every movement!

She thanked him with chilly politeness, sighing resignedly as she closed the door after he had gone. She was over-reacting—letting the man get under her skin. Blade Ryan was hardly responsible for the weather, or for her having to cool her heels in Sydney for a few hours. Had it remained fine, they would have been well on their way to Windarra Valley by now.

She wandered to the window and peered out, but could see nothing through the rain-swept windows but a bleary greyness, the blanket of rain dimming the outline of the tall buildings opposite. Was this sunny Australia? she wondered ruefully. Where was the beautiful Sydney harbour she had heard so much about? Even flying in earlier, she had seen nothing, the cloud cover had concealed everything but the approach to the airport.

By the time she had selected a change of clothes from the smaller of her two suitcases, taken a quick refreshing shower—first cautiously locking the door of the tiny bathroom—and dressed again in the uncrushable blue knit dress she had decided to wear to lunch, Blade Ryan was already waiting for her in the lounge, his muscular frame sprawled in one of the deep armchairs, his long legs stretched out in front of him.

He rose as she walked across the room. Her stomach did a slow somersault as his startling grey eyes slid languidly over her. His hair, almost dry now, was brushed back from his tanned face, a few damp tendrils curling defiantly over his ears and into the nape of his neck. His pale oyster shirt was open at the throat, revealing a tangle of fine hairs and a disturbing glimpse of bronzed flesh.

His gaze completed its lazy inspection and lifted to her face, dwelling a moment on her lips before moving with the same deliberate slowness up the smooth line of her cheek to her eyes. She met his gaze steadily, showing none of the

emotion she felt churning inside her, refusing to acknowledge even to herself that this man, this stranger, could be
responsible for her thudding heart, her racing pulse. She
was tired, jet-lagged. Otherwise she would feel nothing but
irritation that he was looking at her in such a way. She
would despise him. She *did* despise him!

Blade Ryan spoke at last, his voice a low, derisive drawl.
'You're the image of your mother,' he said, and paused.
'Are you alike in other ways too, I wonder?'

Kelly's eyes flared momentarily. Deliberately ignoring
the question and the disparaging undertone, she asked
curiously, 'You remember my mother—from when she was
here in Australia?'

His mouth curved faintly, accentuating the cynical lines
that ran along either side. 'Your mother wasn't a woman
anyone—even a ten-year-old boy—would easily forget.
And judging by the odd Press photograph I've seen since,
the years have barely changed her. I've seen none of her
films though.' He wasn't apologising. It was just a statement
of fact. Blade Ryan didn't strike her as the kind of man who
would apologise for anything. 'I don't often go to the
movies,' he confessed. And when he did, Kelly had the
feeling it would be to see something a bit more meaty than
the schmaltzy roles her mother favoured. 'She's a stun-
ningly beautiful woman,' Blade said levelly, his eyes still on
her face.

Kelly felt a tell-tale rise of colour at the implied
compliment. And yet it was a compliment she had heard
before, countless times . . . and in the past she had always
managed to brush it off, usually rather impatiently. She
didn't want to look like her mother—never had wanted to.
It had led to far too many hassles.

Kelly sighed, turning away to avoid Blade Ryan's
discomfiting gaze. It was *she*, not her mother, who had
chosen—*insisted*—on her staying out of the public glare; she
had wanted nothing to do with the glittering film world, or
with the publicity that surrounded her mother. Her passion
for horses had developed at a very early age. 'I've always
been terrified of horses myself,' Rowena used to complain

half laughingly, half ruefully, to her friends, 'and Chuck wouldn't know one end of a horse from the other!' Her love of horses was in her blood, of course, though nobody spoke of it. Most people wouldn't even have known.

She was tempted to voice her thoughts aloud, but diffidence, or perhaps loyalty to her mother, kept her silent. *Are you alike in other ways too, I wonder?* Blade Ryan had said, and there had been a cold edge to his voice, Kelly recalled. What lay behind it? Hostility? Resentment? Was his disapproval directed at her, for not trying to see her father—her *real* father—in his lifetime? Or at Chuck and Rowena for denying Mungo Heath his only child? How could she explain that Rowena and Chuck had wanted to protect her—to protect their precious family unit? That had been the most important thing in their minds—more important than Mungo Heath, far away in remote Australia, a man who had bitterly rejected all three of them, who had willingly given up all rights to his child; a man they had thought was out of their lives for good.

She felt a strong urge to ask Blade Ryan about Mungo Heath—about her father. Blade had known him, he had said earlier, perhaps better than anybody. She turned back to face him, saw the way he was still scrutinising her—quizzically, coldly, as though he were weighing her, summing her up, and the questions she wanted to ask died in her throat. Perhaps over lunch . . .

'I'll take my umbrella,' she said, casting around for a diversion, and at the same time reminding him that they were going out. 'Do you have one?'

'I'll share yours,' he said with a brief smile, reaching for his jacket, which he had draped over the back of a chair.

That fleeting smile had a surprising effect on Kelly. She felt a prickle of tiny hairs rising at the nape of her neck, while at the same time a shivery sensation feathered down her spine. Until now she hadn't considered him particularly handsome—not in the conventional sense. His attraction, and she couldn't deny it existed, lay in the heavily fringed grey eyes, in his powerful physique, in the aura of easy authority that clung to him. And yet when that

faint smile tugged at his lips, fleeting though it was, the
change it made was startling. She found herself wanting to
see him smile again—a real smile this time, one that
lingered and gave her a chance to explore the changes it
made to his face. She wanted to examine his face as he had
examined hers, and watch the way his smile turned his grey
eyes to molten silver and introduced intriguing creases and
crinkles that hadn't been there previously.

She pulled herself up sharply. You certainly *are* suffering
from jet-lag, Kelly Nagle. Kelly Nagle *Heath*, she mentally
corrected herself. She had decided from now on to adopt
Mungo Heath's surname, to proclaim to his friends, and to
the world, that she was his daughter—and proud of it. She
wasn't herself . . . she needed a good long sleep. Anyway,
his smile had gone now, wiped away as if it had never been.
He was regretting it already, no doubt. He resented her
coming here; he was looking after her under sufferance.
She wasn't sure *why* he resented her so much, unless it was
because of her mother; because he thought she was like
her—flighty, fickle, not to be trusted.

Blade rang for a taxi and they headed for the lift, Kelly
firmly clutching her umbrella, rather as a child clutches its
mother's hand. She sighed as she realised it, deliberately
slackening her grip. Blade Ryan was having a most
peculiar effect on her, and she didn't like it. She didn't like
it one bit. It made her feel vulnerable and weak and unsure
of herself—and that was a new feeling to her, one she had
no wish to give in to. No *intention* of giving in to.

It was still raining outside, more a steady drizzle now,
with occasional sharp gusts of wind. With the aid of the
umbrella they reached the taxi without getting more than a
few spots on them. On their way to the restaurant, they
kept their talk impersonal, Blade pointing out special
landmarks through the grey veil of rain and apologising for
the weather—without looking or sounding the least bit
apologetic. Kelly eyed him suspiciously. Was Blade Ryan
secretly pleased that she was seeing the place in such a poor
light? Was he hoping it would drive her away, back across
the Pacific where she belonged?

It was her uncertainty rather than the rain that caused a sudden dampening of her spirits. Why should Blade Ryan be so anxious for her to leave? She shrugged, trying rather irritably to pull herself together. She must be mistaken, surely. Her strange reaction to the man, part-attraction, part-hostility, was making her ultra-sensitive.

At the restaurant they were given an upstairs table, by a window. Kelly's first glimpse of Sydney Harbour was disappointing. The rain, swept by the strong winds, was beating against the windows, blurring what on a fine day would undoubtedly have been a magnificent view of the harbour and the towering Sydney Harbour Bridge. Between showers she could make out a few murky shapes, but it was a dismal scene. An occasional ferry-boat, barely visible through the grey mist, chugged past, while the opposite bank was blotted out entirely, covered in a bleak slate-coloured shroud.

It was Blade, surprisingly, not she, who first brought up Mungo Heath's name, as they were sipping their pre-lunch orange drinks. Kelly had happily gone along with Blade when he said he didn't drink alcohol before flying a plane.

'I'm sorry Mungo died before you could meet,' Blade said. The words were comforting, but his tone was cold. Again she sensed an unspoken criticism.

She looked at him hard for a moment. 'You knew my father,' she began carefully, and paused, sucking in her breath. 'Do you know why he decided to leave Windarra Stud to me? I always thought he didn't care about me. We all did. He gave me up without a fight before I was even born.'

Blade didn't answer at once. When he did, his voice was toneless, giving no clue to what he was thinking.

'Your mother couldn't have known him very well if she believed he didn't care. He never got over losing you—or your mother. He loved her and he would have loved you too if your mother had stayed. He was devastated when she left him.'

'Devastated?' Kelly echoed dubiously. 'My mother said he acted as if he hated her—she always said his pride was hurt more than his heart. He called her some terrible names, she said, and then he wiped his hands of both of us.'

Blade said scathingly, 'Didn't it occur to her that he was lashing out to hide the hurt he was feeling? Didn't it occur to her that it was because he still loved her that he turned his back on *you*? He wanted to see her happy—and that meant giving *you* up too, to Chuck Nagle, and never trying to interfere. Anyway, seeing you only occasionally would have been too painful—it would have kept the old wounds open. Mungo decided that if he couldn't have Rowena, he wanted nothing more to do with her—or with you. He told me so not long before he died.'

'My mother always said he hated both of us,' Kelly said in a subdued voice. 'He never came near us, he never tried to contact *me*. I came to believe it was true. I'm sure my mother believed it too.'

'He *was* bitter for a long time.' The cool grey eyes were guarded, neither condemning nor sympathetic. 'He couldn't bear to talk about her or hear her name mentioned. But he loved her to the day he died; he never let another woman get close to him. He lived for his horses and his racing. In his own way I think he was happy. No,' he corrected, the cynical lines round his mouth deepening, 'not happy. Content.'

Kelly swallowed. 'And—and what about me?' she asked huskily. 'What made him change his mind and—and acknowledge me as his daughter? Simply because he had no other living relative?'

'I think it was more than that.' Blade's tone was still aloof; his eyes still hooded. 'In recent years he read about your show-jumping successes in his horse magazines, and from time to time in the newspapers. Then one day he saw your photograph on the front cover of a fashion magazine—the one I mentioned earlier. My mother had left it lying on a coffee-table and he saw it when he came to visit. Seeing that photograph, and reading about you and your life with horses, left him visibly shaken. He could see that you were the image of your mother—and yet you had *his* love of horses. To him, you combined everything he had

ever wanted in your mother.' There was a dryness in
Blade's tone that suggested he didn't agree; that he
considered his friend had grown foolishly idealistic with
age. 'He decided to invite you to come and visit him, some
time when you were free of engagements. He wanted you to
see Windarra. But he delayed—pride, uncertainty, fear of
a rebuff, who knows?—and then it was too late. He had
his fatal heart-attack—he had already had a couple of
warnings and had made out his will in your favour. It was a
tragedy. He died a lonely man—unnecessarily.'

There was censure in Blade's voice now, a harshness, a
coldness that cut her to the bone. Did he think she didn't
feel anything for Mungo Heath, simply because she had
never known him, had never met him face to face? Her
heart was crying inside at all those lost years, the years
when she had been busy carving out a career for herself,
little knowing that a proud, lonely man in Australia was
following her career by reading newspapers and horse
magazines. Her *father* . . . the man she had always thought
didn't care about her, the man who had given her up in
anger and seeming indifference before she was born. How
foolish people can be, she thought with a sigh. How blind
and foolish.

She looked down at the plate of prawns and oysters a
waitress had placed in front of her. At the same time Blade
was pouring cider into her glass, and she studied that too,
composing herself before she spoke.

'You seem to be blaming us—me, my mother, Chuck.
And yet we had no idea how Mung—how my father felt.
How could we? He had told my mother he never wanted to
see her or any of us again.'

'When people are deeply hurt they hide behind anger
and say things they don't mean.' The harshness of Blade's
words—the truth of them—made Kelly flinch
involuntarily.

She lifted her chin defiantly, hiding her pain. 'He knew
where to find me—if he had really wanted to.'

'And you knew where to find him—if *you* had wanted to.'

'I didn't think he'd——' she began, and clamped her lips

shut. Why bother to defend herself to this man, to this hostile, righteous stranger? Mungo Heath had been his friend, true, but he had been *her* father. If only Blade Ryan knew how she was grieving inside for the father she had never had a chance to know!

Blade Ryan raised his glass of cider to his lips. 'It must have come as quite a shock,' he murmured smoothly, 'to learn that Mungo Heath, the father you never sought out or bothered to get to know, had left you his entire fortune.'

Her head snapped back sharply. 'It *was* a shock,' she agreed, ignoring the condemnation that lay behind the observation. Now, it seemed, the gloves were off in earnest! 'It meant——' she stopped, blinking away a suspicion of moisture from her eyes. Why bother to tell Blade Ryan how much the gesture had meant to her? He would never understand. He wouldn't *try* to understand.

He was watching her closely. His hand reached across the table and rested for a moment on hers. Fighting back her emotion, she found herself staring at it, examining the spread of veins across its back and the fine hairs sprouting from the tanned skin.

'Let's leave it there,' Blade said in a gentler tone. 'I guess I shouldn't blame you. You never knew him. If anyone's to blame——' he let the words trail away, his shoulders lifting and falling, apparently thinking twice about saying what was on the tip of his tongue.

She became still, her eyes contracting, taking on a deeper violet hue. 'Yes?' she said, forcing the question out. He meant her mother, of course. Rowena Shaw . . . the scarlet woman . . . the villain of the piece, in his eyes. He still blamed her, twenty-five years after the event!

When he didn't speak at once, she answered for him. 'You mean my mother. My mother,' she went on steadily, 'would be the first to admit that she made a mistake when she married Mungo Heath. She wasn't suited to the life out here; but she did try—and kept on trying . . . until she met Chuck Nagle. They had a lot in common and they fell in love. It does happen, you know,' she said with heavy sarcasm. 'She and Chuck have been happily married now for nearly twenty-five years. Chuck——' she stopped abruptly. What in the world was she doing, justifying her mother's past actions, Chuck's actions, to this stranger, this—this *neighbour*? 'I really don't see that it's any of your business,' she said impatiently.

'You're right, of course.' His hand left hers abruptly, leaving her feeling strangely chilled—and yet relieved at the same time. Leaving her feeling oddly confused.

She stifled a sigh, looking down at her glass to hide her emotions from his all-too-perceptive gaze. She didn't know what she felt any more. Blade Ryan was a thoroughly perplexing, annoying, disconcerting, infuriating man. A dangerous man, something in her bones told her. If she were to keep a cool head and her wits about her she would be wise to keep him at arm's length.

CHAPTER TWO

BLADE rose from the table, motioning to her to stay where she was. 'Excuse me for a moment, I want to make a couple of phone-calls.' When he came back a few minutes later he told her the storm had passed over the airport and the air-traffic was moving again.

'I've been in contact with Windarra Stud as well. The storm passed over there earlier. It's still misty, but it's clearing. I think we'll chance it. It may be a bumpy ride though, but don't worry, I'll get you there in one piece.'

He looked down at her, as though waiting for a reaction. She met his gaze coolly. Did he expect her to cringe in fear at the prospect of a rough ride? If so, he would be disappointed!

She started gathering up her umbrella and handbag. 'Good. I'm ready. Let's go.'

He waved her back, an expression she couldn't read flickering across his face. 'I've ordered coffee. Plenty of time. Our cab won't be here for twenty minutes.'

As he slid back into the seat opposite, the waitress arrived with two steaming cups of cappuccino. Blade offered Kelly sugar and took some himself.

'So. . .' He sat back, regarding her obliquely over the rim of his cup. 'You've taken a break from show-jumping to come out and look over your inheritance.'

She took a long careful breath. How could she explain to Blade Ryan that she wanted to do more than just 'look the place over'? She wanted to stay awhile and get to know the valley, to learn to love it the way her father had. She wanted to work alongside the people he had worked alongside and get to know them, and let them get to know her. Blade Ryan's assumption that she was not planning to stay long in the valley—let alone stay for good—raised a flare of rebellion inside her. Whether she stayed or not—

stayed *permanently*—would depend on a whole host of things: on her empathy with the place and with the people who worked there, on her own capabilities, on what precisely was involved in the running of a top thorough-bred stud in Australia. How would she know until she had spent some time there? In the meantime she wasn't going to be steam-rollered into making an early decision, one way or the other.

'I'm looking for a new challenge,' she told him seriously. 'Show-jumping just doesn't have the appeal it used to. I've been in it for a long time. And now that I've lost Pixie . . .' She shrugged, looking down at her coffee to hide her pain. There were other reasons too, but she wasn't going to mention Harvey Quinn to Blade Ryan. 'It's time I tried something else. Show-jumping has been my whole life until now—but the show-jumping world isn't everything—not by a long way. I want to broaden my horizons.'

Now for the first time, his face showed clearly what he was feeling. Consternation. 'You're thinking of giving up show-jumping for *good*? You must have years ahead of you! How old are you? Twenty-two? Twenty-three?'

'Twenty-four.' She kept her voice as impassive as her expression.

'Quite.' His metallic eyes slid arrogantly over her.

'I've been at the top of my field for years now,' she heard herself retorting with equal arrogance. 'I started very young. It's a young person's profession, Mr Ryan.'

'You were calling me Blade before.'

'Blade, then. There are other things in life than show-jumping,' she said, parodying Blade's earlier remark about there being 'other things in life than Bilba'.

'Very true,' he drawled, and spread his hands as he conceded, 'it must get pretty exhausting at times, with all the travelling and the hours of training involved. I guess there comes a time when you want to settle down to a quiet life. You'll be a wealthy woman when you sell Windarra Stud, you'll be able to afford a string of show-jumpers back in the States—and someone to do all the hard work for you. Or does a more domestic life-style have a greater appeal?

Marriage, children?'

She ignored that. Chauvinist pig, she thought acidly. *When* you sell Windarra Stud, he had said. Not *if* you sell. The gall of the man!

And now it was out in the open. Blade Ryan did expect her to go back to the States. Or *hoped* she would. Just as Rowena did. Her mother had been against her even flying out to look Windarra Stud over.

'Who said I'm going back?' she hedged, and she swung her head round to gaze out across the misty harbour. The rain had stopped at last and the overcast sky was definitely lightening. Boats and buildings she hadn't seen before were taking shape out of the greyness. She kept her face averted, not wanting to see that same incredulous look on Blade's face that she had seen on her mother's. She knew it would be there. Perhaps irritation too, in Blade Ryan's case. She wished she knew *why* he should feel irritated, *why* he was so against her staying. Because she was a woman? A foreigner?

'We understood you would be selling Windarra,' Blade said at length. The very calmness of his voice told her instinctively that he was not as calm as he made out. 'We were surprised to hear you were coming out in person, especially at such short notice. We expected you to send someone to act on your behalf.'

'To act on my behalf?' she repeated coldly. Rowena had said much the same thing.

'To arrange the sale.'

She met him eye to eye. 'You think I intend to sell Windarra Stud?'

'Well, don't you?' Their eyes locked together, startling grey warring with rebellious violet. It was he, surprisingly, who dropped his gaze first, allowing his dark-fringed lashes to flicker downwards to veil the impact of the intense grey as he reached languidly for his coffee.

She sensed that he was waiting very intently for her reply. *Why?* Because he didn't want to see a woman running the neighbouring stud? Or was it that he didn't want *Rowena Shaw's daughter* to be his new neighbour?

Or was he simply concerned about the property of his old friend, Mungo Heath, anxious to know who was going to run it, and who his new neighbour was likely to be?

In a strange, almost chilling way, she felt she was being manipulated in some fashion, led along a path of Blade Ryan's choosing—and that they had now reached the point to which he had been relentlessly steering her.

Well, Blade Ryan, she thought as he glanced up again, as their eyes clashed for the second time; you will find out I am not so easy to manipulate.

'You sound like my mother,' she said coolly.

He didn't like that. Though not a muscle of his face so much as twitched, she sensed that he didn't like being compared with Rowena. Knowing of old how irritated she had felt herself whenever she was likened to her mother, she smiled to herself, feeling she had scored a small point over her arrogant neighbour.

He seemed to catch her smile and interpret it, his eyes narrowing speculatively, glinting with the coldness of old pewter. But his voice, when he spoke, was bland.

'I think your mother's given you sound advice. You don't really want to uproot yourself and leave all your friends and the only family you've ever known——'

She cut in sharply, her cheeks afire. 'You're forgetting, aren't you, that part of my family lived *here*—here in Australia—and that I never had a chance to know him, or his home and surroundings.'

Shutters immediately came down over his eyes. He backed down at once—if only partially. Just enough to make her suspicious. A man like Blade Ryan, something warned her, didn't back down without a good reason.

'Well, naturally you'd want to stay here awhile and have a good look over the place where the father you never knew lived. But he's not here any longer,' he pointed out with a brutal logic that caused her lips to tighten. 'It will hardly be the same, will it? However, if you sell to the right person, you need have no fear that what Mungo Heath built up in Windarra Valley will be lost—in any way.'

'The right person?' Her eyes flared, her mistrust

deepening. 'And who might the right person be? Obviously you have someone in mind.'

His lips moved ever so slightly; not a smile, but perhaps intended as one.

'My sister Megan is marrying Dan Cassidy, our stud-groom, early in the New Year—after things quieten down at Bilba.'

'*He* wants to buy Windarra Stud?' It made sense, of course, that Bilba's stud-groom would want a place of his own after his marriage. But could he afford *Windarra*? The Ryans would help him, no doubt. After all, he was marrying into the family.

She was surprised when Blade shook his head. 'Not Dan, no. Dan wants to stay on at Bilba, he wants to *run* Bilba, in fact. The cottage he's in at present, though, is really too small for a wife and family. If I moved out of the family home, he and Megan could move in there.'

Kelly found she was hardly breathing. 'Why should you move out of your own home?' she asked, forcing the question out.

'We want to extend our operations beyond Bilba Valley,' Blade answered quietly. 'I've been on the lookout for a suitable property, ideally with a house already on the land.'

Kelly caught her breath. *Blade Ryan wanted Windarra Stud!* Why, oh why, hadn't she guessed it earlier? Why else would he have offered to come and pick her up? Why else would he have backed down a moment ago—and pretended to agree with her earlier when she said that a weekend stay would not be long enough? Blade Ryan was not the kind of man to back down to a woman—she had guessed that from the start! Why else would he have wanted her all to himself, away from the bustle of the airport—away from the intrusion of reporters and camera-men? He hadn't been thinking of her at all. He had been thinking only of what he could pluck from her!

Her voice, when she answered, was surprisingly calm. 'So the Ryans have Bilba Valley all sewn up, and now they want Windarra Valley as well. With Windarra Stud thrown in!'

He met her cool gaze steadily, replying with a calm to
match hers, 'That's right. Don't worry, I assure you we'll
pay a good price. Better than you'd get from anyone else.
You won't lose out.'

He sounded so confident. So insufferably confident!

'Naturally, we'd like to put in an offer for Mungo's light
plane too—and for his racehorse Heathcote, if you intend
to sell him.' The smouldering grey eyes burned into her
own, and angry as she was, she felt herself shaking under
their impact. 'He'll be ready for stud soon, and as a Derby
winner he'll attract only the best mares. If you wish to
retain a part-share in the horse, we'd have no objection.'

Kelly gasped. No objection! How kind of him!

She waited a moment before she spoke, composing
herself, trying to stay calm, though her heart was quivering
with outraged anger—and a frustration she had seldom
experienced. Hadn't she sensed that this man was
dangerous? And he was strong, too—strong-*willed*—a man
used to having his own way, if she had read all the signs
correctly. But so was she. She had never bowed to a man
yet—against her will. And she didn't intend to bow to
Blade Ryan!

'Surely if my father had wanted you to have Windarra
Stud—or his racehorse Heathcote—he would have speci-
fied in his will that I should sell to you.'

Blade didn't answer at once and her eyes gleamed with
triumph as she mentally scored another point. Scoring
points over Blade Ryan, she thought wryly, would not
happen easily or often.

At length he answered in a mocking drawl, his eyes
holding hers captive, so that she was vividly aware of every
tiny fleck in the molten grey. 'I guess he was relying on my
powers of persuasion.'

She drew back sharply, tugging her eyes away from his,
as angry at herself as at him, realising that she had fallen
into a trap of Blade Ryan's making. He had set out
deliberately to weaken her defences by using those
powerful eyes of his, and he had almost succeeded.

Almost, but not quite! 'I don't allow other people to

influence my decisions—particularly a person I barely know,' she said frigidly, reaching for her bag. 'I think your twenty minutes are up. Thank you for the lunch.'

She happened to glance inadvertently at his face as she rose, and was shaken to see that, far from being angry, far from being discouraged, he appeared to be amused. He looked on this as a game, an amusing challenge, no doubt. Well, she could play games too, and she had the killer instinct needed to win!

The sky was still overcast when they took off in the Piper Cherokee, with Blade settled comfortably at the controls and Kelly seated stiffly beside him. The wind buffeted the tiny plane as it rose into the sky, drawing a laconic apology from Blade.

'Warned you it might be a bit rough. We often have erratic winds in Australia, especially in the tail of a storm.' There was a hint of exultation in his voice. He was enjoying it, she realised, watching breathlessly as he threaded the plane through the low clouds. Was he enjoying the danger? The exhilaration? Or enjoying having her at his mercy!

'I've been on rougher trips than this,' she returned breezily—though never, she added to herself, in a plane as tiny as this one. Blade seemed a competent pilot, though, thoroughly at ease at the controls. 'You say flying is one of your passions?' she recalled aloud.

'Pardon?' Blade inclined his head slightly. 'Flying is what?'

'One of your *passions*,' she shouted back, over the roar of the engine.

'Oh, *passions*!' His lips moved, and she felt a blush sweep across her face. She hissed in her breath, angry at the way he had tricked her into repeating the word, angry at herself too, for colouring up like an impressionable schoolgirl.

'Yes, flying is a passion of mine.' He wasn't looking at her, thank goodness; his eyes were fixed ahead. 'I used to fly light planes often while I was studying to be a vet, and during the three years I practised. After that I gave up my veterinary practice to become an airline pilot.'

'An airline pilot!' Kelly blinked at him in surprise.

She saw his lip quirk upwards. 'Variety, so they say, is the spice of life. I was an airline pilot up until four years ago, when my father died and I came back to Bilba to take charge. I'd always spent my holidays and time off at Bilba, apart from a couple of extended vacations I spent overseas visiting the top stud-farms, studying breeding methods and veterinary practice. I've been lucky—I've had the best of both worlds.'

'You don't miss your glamorous life as an airline pilot?' she asked, injecting a bantering note to mask her curiosity, and deliberately using the word 'glamorous' in retaliation for his scathing remark earlier about her own 'glamorous' life and 'glamorous' connections.

'Not at all.' His eyelids flickered slightly, as though acknowledging the barb. 'I always intended to retire early and come back to the valley.' His voice sobered. 'With my father gone, I've had full responsibility for running Bilba, and it's a life I wouldn't want to swap for any other. I can still fly when I want to, in fact light planes are a vital part of our existence. Anyway, I told you, flying is only *one* of my passions. Horses are the other. Horses, and of course . . .' his gaze flicked round, his voice taunting, 'beautiful women are another.'

Though he spoke lightly, intending it as a joke, the cynicism in his voice didn't escape her. She frowned, her teeth digging into her lip. He didn't think much of beautiful women—that was obvious. They might attract his eye, but she doubted whether Blade Ryan would ever place them on a pedestal or grovel at their feet—or even particularly like them. He would use them for his own purpose—as *playthings*, she suspected, and then callously discard them. Or maybe he kept half a dozen on a string, caring nothing for any of them.

'I take it you're not married, Mr Ryan,' she said icily.

He laughed aloud, and she sensed that behind the blue-tinted sunglasses his eyes were mocking her.

'No, I've managed to avoid that blessed state so far. I'd have to be very sure before I committed the rest of my natural life to one woman.' His tone was sardonic, and there was an arrogant curl to his well shaped lips. 'Besides, only a special kind of woman would want to settle down to domestic bliss in an isolated spot like Bilba. It's not an easy life. It would take a woman with guts—with the necessary moral fibre and physical stamina—to be able to take it and stick it out.'

And stick it out. Kelly sucked in her breath. He was thinking of her mother, of course, walking out on Mungo Heath and Windarra. And it was plain that he equated her, Kelly, with her mother. She tossed him a vitriolic look. Why didn't he come right out and say it? That he didn't expect her to stay in Australia, that he didn't *want* her to stay, that because he wanted Windarra Stud for himself he was going to do his best to *discourage* her from staying!

'Your mother and sister seem to thrive on the life, by all accounts,' she retorted tartly, wondering why she was bothering to argue with him. Blade Ryan had no influence over her. None at all. He could try as hard as he pleased to dampen her enthusiasm, but she would make up her own mind whether she stayed or not.

'My mother and sister are a rare breed.' His voice had sharpened. 'They're strong—women of backbone. They support their men. Words like loyalty and fidelity mean something to them.'

Kelly bit back a gasp. He was sniping at her mother again, and in the same breath he seemed to be implying that she, Kelly, would turn out to be as fickle, as unstable as he saw her mother.

Blade glanced down suddenly at the tilting earth. 'Look down—now!' he commanded.

As Kelly twisted her head round to look out of the window, the cry that escaped her lips was a spontaneous cry of sheer delight.

They were flying over a broad sweeping plain, fresh and gleaming after the rain—a patchwork of lush green and soft brown squares, criss-crossed with unsealed roads and neat white-railed fences. Rising steeply from the timbered side gullies towered rugged sandstone cliffs, indigo in the hazy afternoon.

'It's breath-taking,' she breathed. 'Is it——?'

'Windarra Valley,' Blade confirmed. 'Windarra Stud directly below.' Something in his voice—almost a caressing note—made her wonder if it had been the prospect of seeing Windarra Stud, and not the flight itself, which had brought the exhilaration to his voice. Windarra Stud . . . the glittering prize he coveted!

She was momentarily dazzled by a glint of sunlight on galvanised iron. She caught a glimpse of other buildings, half hidden by a curtain of deep green. A river, like a silvery snake, meandered behind the sprawling stable complex, lithe drooping willows softening its banks. Small brown blobs became horses, moving dots became long-legged foals, frisking in the succulent paddocks beside their mothers.

'We're going in,' Blade shouted. The plane banked sharply and went into a swooping dive, Kelly's stomach swooping with it. The runway of the Windarra airstrip rushed to meet them—surely it was coming up too fast! Was he trying to frighten her to death? She braced herself for a rough landing.

The wheels touched the runway with barely a thud. A hotshot landing, she had to admit. He certainly was a superb pilot.

As he taxied the machine to a halt near a galvanised-iron shed at the end of the runway, he patted the control panel with something close to affection.

'I think the old Cherokee enjoyed that,' he muttered with satisfaction. 'It's a nice little plane. Joe only flies occasionally, but Mungo used to fly it a lot, for business trips and on race days.'

'This is my father's plane?' Kelly asked slowly. She couldn't bring herself to say 'mine', but the word hung unspoken in the air. What was Blade Ryan doing flying Mungo Heath's plane? The plane he had already told her he wanted to buy, along with Windarra Stud and the racehorse Heathcote and all her father's stallions, mares, foals, yearlings, cattle, and his house thrown in!

Blade looked unruffled. 'We thought a run would do it good. I came over yesterday and picked it up. I've been spending quite a lot of time here at Windarra since Mungo died, helping Joe out. The breeding and foaling season is always a hectic time.'

As he unfolded his long frame and reached across to open the door, Kelly's eyes flared with swift anger. So, he had started moving in already, had he? Just waiting for his chance to sign on the dotted line and officially take over everything!

She fought down the bitter retort that sprang to her lips. She must keep her head.

'That was very kind of you,' she said in cool clipped tones. 'I appreciate your giving Joe a hand until I arrived.' She spoke dismissively, emphasising the words *until I arrived*.

'You're welcome.' His lips twitched as though he found her reaction amusing. This was all a game to him. He was so confident of winning!

As he helped her down from the plane, her heels sank into the rain-softened earth and she was glad she had chosen sensible shoes with medium heels. After hauling down her two suitcases, Blade led her to a Land Rover parked near the shed.

'Yours?' she asked drily, and he nodded, fine lines radiating from his eyes. He threw her bags into the back of the vehicle and strode round to open the passenger door for her, reaching past her to brush the seat with an exaggerated flick of his hand.

'It's a bit dusty—she's been sitting out here for two days. Be thankful I didn't leave the windows open, you'd be sitting in a puddle of muddy water.'

'It's fine,' she said shortly. Was he deliberately trying to disenchant her with his talk of dust and muddy puddles?

'First stop, the homestead,' Blade said, sliding into the driver's seat beside her.

They drove between lush green paddocks, neatly fenced. Placid mares lifted their heads curiously as they drove by, and scruffy-coated foals kicked up their heels, the smaller ones wobbling about on long ungainly legs, their tiny faces alert.

'There are about a hundred thoroughbred mares here at the moment, with their foals,' Blade told her, and for once the cynicism was absent from his voice. 'Some are Heath-owned, the rest are visiting mares. The foals are delightful, aren't they?' And then came the sting. 'Sadly, about half the annual crop of thoroughbreds never manage to achieve the purpose for which they were bred—namely, to win races. So many things can go wrong, premature death, accidents, unsoundness, virus infection, or simply because they're not fast enough. The mares have their own set of problems.' Kelly held her breath, waiting for sting number two. 'Despite all the advances in veterinary science, the sobering fact remains that one mare in three overall fails to produce a foal every year.'

'I realise the problems,' Kelly said levelly. 'I've been involved with horses for a long time, remember? Ex-racehorses among them. I've done advanced courses in horsemanship as well—stable management, ailments and diseases, handling horses, training methods, the whole lot ... and I've done business studies too—book-keeping, accounting, computer science——'

'I'm sure your background is impeccable,' he said with a sardonic lift of his lip. Sensing that a 'but' was coming, Kelly hastened on.

'Perhaps I don't know much yet about breeding racehorses—especially here in Australia—but I'm keen to learn. I'm *determined* to learn. I intend to read up on all the literature, and talk to people, and observe and absorb everything there is to know. As well as involve myself in the actual physical work.

As she paused for breath he interjected with a low chuckle, 'My, I did disturb a hornet's nest!' His tone was teasing, with a patronising note that secretly incensed her. 'I wasn't reflecting on your capabilities, Kelly, I assure you. Merely pointing out some cold hard facts. You'll be burying your head in the sand if you ignore them. You'll find we do things differently here in Australia. I don't mean simply that we breed at a different time of the year, but our foaling methods, for example, are different—we foal out in the open, not in heated stables. And we don't treat our young horses like precious glassware—we believe in shifting them out of their lush grasslands on to tougher country, so they can stretch out and gallop over rises and rough it a bit as they're growing up.'

'Thank you, I'm obliged to you,' said Kelly, and despite a touch of sarcasm she realised she could learn a lot from this man. But would he be willing to teach her? He didn't expect her to stay long. He didn't *want* her to stay—he wanted to buy her out. Why should he make things easier for her?

'I guess what I'm trying to say,' Blade went on, a serious note entering his voice, 'is don't be too carried away by the glamour of the place. It *is* beautiful, especially at this time of year, with the new foals and everything green and succulent and looking great. But in a couple of months, when the summer heat dries those lush hills and gullies, we'll have a new worry—bushfires. Bilba was almost wiped out once, in my grandfather's time. These are the things you should keep in mind.'

'I'm sure everything you say is one hundred per cent accurate,' Kelly said sweetly. 'You're sounding more like my mother every minute,' she added, knowing that would hurt. '*She* gave me a lot of cold, hard facts too—in fact she painted almost as daunting a picture as you have. She too warned me not to let the beauty of the place sweep me off my feet. Wasn't I lucky to have you with me to keep my feet firmly on the ground?'

'You were indeed,' he said tartly. 'As long as they *are* on the ground, go ahead and enjoy . . .' she thought he was going to say *your stay*, but he must have decided on discretion, this once. 'Enjoy the place.'

'Thank you,' she said in the same honeyed tone. 'You mean there are actually things to enjoy?'

'Naturally.' His tone was derisive now. She had angered him, had actually managed to pierce that iron-hard exterior. 'If there weren't some compensations and rewards,

nobody would take on the life.' After a pause he added
gravely, 'Our greatest reward is the sight of a healthy new-
born foal ... that's what makes it all worthwhile.'

She glanced at him in surprise. His tone had changed. He
was making a simple, sincere statement of fact. She was not
only surprised, but curiously pleased that Blade Ryan,
ambitious and arrogant and ruthless as he appeared to be,
should consider the birth of a foal, and not any hard
monetary gain, to be his greatest reward.

'Not one of your horses winning the Derby or the
Melbourne Cup?' she challenged. And thought, what am I
doing—*testing* him?

His eyebrow shot up. Cynicism curved his lips. She
realised even before he spoke that he had taken the question
the wrong way. 'Naturally, winning races is important. It's
what we're all about, isn't it?' His sarcasm made her cringe
inwardly. 'That's why we study blood-lines and facts and
figures—because we're trying to produce the perfect
racehorse. It's a scientific business. But there *is* a human side
too. Homestead coming up,' he said curtly, dismissing the
subject.

Instantly her grievances were forgotten. They had
passed through an open gateway into a long gravel drive
flanked by slender poplars which, closer to the house, gave
way to flowering cherries in delicate blossom, fragrant
lilacs, and golden wattles, their branches spectacular with
clusters of brilliant yellow ball-like flowers. Up ahead she
caught a glimpse of ivy-clad brick walls, a red-tiled roof,
shady verandahs and charming small-paned windows.
Windarra homestead! The house where Mungo Heath, her
father, had lived in bitter isolation for so many years.

She gulped back a surge of emotion.

Blade brought the Land Rover to a smooth halt in front
of the wide front steps. The front door opened magically
and a dusky-faced woman in a floral dress appeared, a
plump woman with brown frizzy hair and big brown eyes
that blinked curiously at Blade's passenger.

'Elsie Duncan, Mungo's housekeeper,' Blade murmured.
'You'll never see Elsie hurry or get in a flap, but she gets

things done and you can rely on her absolutely. Her
husband used to work on the stud—he was part-Aboriginal
too—but he died recently and Elsie agreed to stay on.
When we go in you'll meet Mary Lou too, Mungo's private
secretary.' Was she imagining it, or did his eyes soften as he
mentioned the girl's name? 'She comes in each day from
Wattlefield, the local town. I've been giving her a hand—
Joe's been too busy in the stables to keep up with the
business side as well. Anyway, that's not really Joe's forte.'

'I hope you haven't been neglecting Bilba,' Kelly said,
feeling half grateful, half resentful. There was no doubt
about it, Blade Ryan had already moved in! Was he trying
to make himself indispensable?

'We have more staff at Bilba than you have here at
Windarra,' he answered glibly, 'and I have my mother and
sister to do most of our book-work. My mother deals with
visitors and phone-calls when I'm not there, and Dan
Cassidy, my sister's fiancé, is a very competent stud-man—I
can rely on him to keep things running smoothly, with the
lads to help him around the stud.'

She felt like retorting, 'Aren't you lucky?' but she knew it
would sound petty and ungrateful. Besides, she didn't want
to get locked into another clash of wills with Blade Ryan—
she wanted to get out of the car and breathe in the
atmosphere.

'What a magnificent eucalypt,' she said as she clambered
out. The tree stood at the edge of the drive, tall and smooth-
trunked, the sun filtering through its branches, throwing a
dappled pattern on to the gravel.

'We call them gum trees here,' Blade murmured,
reaching for her suitcases.

'Gum trees,' she repeated dreamily. Reaching high, she
plucked a frosty blue sickle-shaped leaf and crushed it
between her fingers. It turned green and sticky. She sniffed
it deeply, and felt a shocking bite of pungency up her
nostrils. She threw it down, grabbed her nose in pain, and
sneezed.

Blade roared with laughter. 'That's what comes of being
a stickybeak,' he said good-humouredly, and she smiled

involuntarily, repeating the word wonderingly.

'Stickybeak? Is that an Australian word too?'

He nodded, smiling down at her, the expression in his eyes masked by his sunglasses. She wondered if it was the thought of seeing the girl called Mary Lou that had put him in such a good humour. Or was it because he was standing on Windarra soil? The soil he hoped to gain possession of! 'Come and meet Elsie,' he said, still smiling.

She swallowed hard. That smile! It was the same smile she had seen once before, ever so fleetingly. It did wonders for his face, she grudgingly admitted, smoothing out the cynical lines and wiping away the derision that was so often there. It did something to her heart as well—and that was something she could not allow! Blade Ryan was the *enemy*— the man who wanted to buy her out. She must keep her wits well and truly about her while Blade Ryan was around, or she would find herself meekly agreeing to hand Windarra Stud over to him and then crawling, defeated, back home. Wouldn't Rowena be pleased if she did! Wouldn't Harvey Quinn! She could already hear him saying 'I knew you'd be back, couldn't keep away from me, could you?' And wouldn't Blade Ryan love it most of all—to see the back of her! He would have everything he wanted, and all she would be left with would be an abundance of cold hard cash and a dim, brief memory of a place she was never going to call her own.

Over my dead body, Blade Ryan, she vowed silently, and the smile that had stupidly lingered on her lips was now directed determinedly, not at Blade Ryan, but at Elsie Duncan, her father's housekeeper.

CHAPTER THREE

FOLLOWING Elsie Duncan through the house, with Blade striding behind with the two suitcases, Kelly had an impression of practicality, solidity and comfort. And a certain drabness, a lack of life. Certainly a lack of colour. Brown leather armchairs, heavy beige curtains, solid oak furniture, exposed brick walls, and scattered skin and wool rugs; a man's world, with all the soft feminine touches that must have been there in Rowena's day painstakingly removed.

It made her feel sad, and yet in a way she understood. Mungo Heath had been bitterly hurt—'devastated', had been Blade Ryan's word—when Rowena left him. It was understandable that Mungo would have tried, for his own peace of mind, to erase all trace of her from his house—and from his memory.

Wide stone archways led from room to room, except in the two-storeyed bedroom wing. Everywhere Kelly was struck by the sombre colours, the light-blocking curtains, the austerity, the lack of living plants or welcoming flowers.

'You're very quiet.' Blade's voice was a deep drone close to her ear. 'Not quite what you were expecting? It's hardly luxurious, I agree, but it *is* comfortable.' His voice implied that it would be comfortable enough, at least, for the limited time she would be there.

She lifted her chin. 'It's a beautiful house, charming. It's a house you could feel wonderfully at home in. I'm not into luxury, houses where everything is so exquisite and delicate you're scared to sit down or touch anything. I like to feel comfortable when I come home.'

She didn't glance round to see how he had taken that. Knowing that she was already thinking of the place as 'home' would be the last thing Blade Ryan would want

46

to hear, she suspected. She pressed home her point.

'It's a little sombre—a few flowers and plants would add a bit of life, and some colourful cushions and lampshades—but those things are easily fixed. I have a few things of my own—lamps, ornaments, artefacts, things like that—I'll have sent out.' She didn't add *if I stay*. Let Blade Ryan stew! 'I'm sure my father would have liked to see something of my own personality in the house he left me—the home he wanted me to have,' she added succinctly.

Blade Ryan's answer was swift and sharp, uttered in a low growl so that Elsie Duncan, shuffling on ahead, could not hear. 'Do you really think your father expected you to *live* here? Can't you get it into your head that he *expected* you to sell up?'

Kelly wheeled, white-faced. 'I don't believe that! You're only saying it because you want to get your greedy hands on everything yourself!'

'Think about it,' he said brutally—not denying the accusation, she noticed. 'Mungo knew full well you were a top international show-jumper with a successful life of your own, and that everything you know and love is in America, not here. Do you honestly believe he would have wanted you to give all that up and come all the way out here, away from your friends and family and your show-jumping world, to breed racehorses in the Australian bush?'

To emphasise his point, he put the suitcases down and swayed over her, gesticulating with his hands. Kelly was dimly aware that Elsie Duncan, somewhere ahead, had vanished into one of the rooms.

'Face it, Kelly——' Blade's eyes were steely under the dark lashes '—leaving you everything he possessed was basically a *gesture*—a pretty remarkable gesture, granted, but you must see why Mungo did it. It was his way of acknowledging you as his daughter, his way of making up to you for not being a father to you or giving you anything *materially* in his lifetime.'

Kelly stared at him for a long moment, her eyes unblinking in the dimness, deepening to purple as he watched.

'No, you're wrong.' Suddenly she saw very clearly what she hadn't seen before. 'That may have been part of it,' she conceded, her eyes burning with a strange new light. 'But I think there's more to it. My father knew I shared his love of horses.' She spoke slowly, wonderingly, feeling her way. 'And by leaving me his home and his stud-farm—*intact*— instead of leaving instructions that part or all of it was to be sold to you or anyone else and simply leaving me the cash from the sale, he was giving me a *choice*, don't you see? The choice to take over here, to come and run the place myself, or to sell up and stay with show-jumping and the world I know, if that's what I prefer.'

She expected Blade Ryan to scoff at the notion, to deny that his friend Mungo Heath had had any such intention. Instead, he bent slowly to retrieve her suitcases, and his eyes in that moment were hidden from her. It was only after he had straightened that he spoke, his tone soft and velvet-smooth, his face impassive. For some inexplicable reason she shivered.

'Who knows?' was all he said. 'My offer still stands. You won't get another offer to match it.'

She sighed, her fists clenching involuntarily. Obviously, he didn't agree; and he preferred to ignore her hints that she might stay. *Why?* Did he honestly believe that she wouldn't be able to stick it out here—even if she decided she wanted to try? Would he be constantly dogging her footsteps, applying the pressure to sell every time they came face to face?

She wasn't going to put up with that! How could she function properly with that kind of pressure hanging over her? No, somehow she would have to fob him off, make some kind of bargain with him to get him off her back until she decided for herself what she wanted to do. Of course, once she decided to stay—*if* she decided to stay—he would have no hope at all—and nothing he did or said would change her mind. He didn't know yet just how determined she could be!

'Look,' she said, without moving, 'I'll tell you what I'm prepared to do. If I do decide to sell, I'll give you first option

to buy . . .' as his eyes flared with a glow of triumph, and
something else that she would have sworn was derision, she
qualified it '. . . if I think it's in the best interests of
Windarra Stud. I don't know enough yet about the set-up
here, or about *you*,' she said bluntly, 'to go further than that
just now. You're the only person I've spoken to so far. I
really know nothing about you—other than what you've
told me yourself. If Joe McQueen and the other people here
at Windarra can vouch for you, I'll keep my bargain.'

'I'm satisfied with that.' His tone was sardonic, his
confidence undimmed. 'More than satisfied.'

'Right. Then we needn't touch on the matter again, need
we?' she said with a toss of her dark hair. Swinging round,
she hastened after Elsie Duncan.

The bedroom where they found Elsie was almost as dark
as the passage, the small-paned windows heavily over-
grown with some kind of creeper that shut out most of the
daylight. The heavy curtains on either side of the window
did nothing to help.

Dim or not, she caught the look Elsie threw at Blade
Ryan—a look of triumph, not unlike Blade's of a moment
ago. Had they planned between them to give her the
smallest, dingiest room in the house? Or were all the
bedrooms like this one? She doubted it, in a house of this
size.

How petty, she thought in disgust. How petty and
despicable! And futile too, since the house belonged to her.
What was to stop her moving into any room she chose? She
resolved to have a good look around the moment they left
her alone, and make up her own mind which room she
wanted.

But Blade Ryan surprised her. 'Why in the world have
you put Kelly in here, Elsie, and not upstairs in one of the
larger rooms?' he demanded, frowning at the housekeeper
until the woman's look of triumph faded to a sulk.

'The rooms down here are handy to everything,' she
mumbled. 'I thought——'

'You thought wrong,' Blade cut in harshly. 'Lead the

way upstairs, Elsie. I'd suggest the room overlooking the
river.'

As Elsie stomped on ahead, Kelly followed thoughtfully.
She might have known Blade Ryan would not be a man to
stoop to such petty, transparent tactics. He wanted to see
her leave Windarra—and he would fight hard for what he
wanted—but he wouldn't adopt puny methods that she
could laugh to scorn, that would ultimately weaken him in
her eyes and give her the upper hand. He would be a tough
opponent, a dangerous opponent, perhaps even a ruthless
one. But never petty, she was sure of that. Not Blade Ryan.
He was far too shrewd for that.

The room Blade had suggested was more than satisfac-
tory. Furnished in shades of blue, with a magnificent
queen-sized brass bed, it was a lighter, brighter room than
the ones she had seen so far; with a view, as Blade had
mentioned, that encompassed the willow-lined banks of the
river. It also overlooked a lawn-tennis court which looked
as though it hadn't been used for some time. The grass was
long and straggly and choked with weeds, and the wire
fence surrounding the court sagged badly in places.

She ran her tongue musingly over her lips before turning
back to face Blade Ryan. Not petty, no, but subtle. Oh yes.
There was a devilishly subtle message in that abandoned
tennis court, suggesting loneliness, neglect—and much-
needed work.

Touché, Blade Ryan. One to you.

'I haven't played tennis for ages,' she said with a bright
smile as Elsie Duncan stripped the bed with unnecessary
vigour. 'Once things quieten down, I must do something
about that court. Perhaps we could have a game some
time?'

Something flashed in Blade Ryan's eyes—like a knife
glinting in the sun, Kelly thought, her smile twisting a
little. A knife he would like to plunge into *her*, no doubt.

Blade ignored the invitation. Instead he drawled,
'Mungo was always too busy to play tennis. The court got
beyond him, I'm afraid.'

Implying that it would get beyond her too?

She should have let it go, but she heard herself speaking out in defence of her father.

'Considering my father's health, I guess a vigorous game of tennis was the last thing he would have wanted to play—so why should he bother to look after the court? Anyway, I believe you said he preferred other forms of recreation. Like going to the races. I won't be doing so much of that myself—unless my father's horse Heathcote happens to be running in an important race.' Her voice trailed off as Blade, having dumped her two suitcases beside the big brass bed, started moving towards the door.

'Heathcote is racing next weekend, as a matter of fact.' Blade paused when he reached the doorway, his head almost touching the frame above. 'He's running in the Caulfield Cup down in Melbourne. I suppose you'll be going down to Melbourne to watch, will you?'

She managed—only just—not to frown, not to show any outward irritation. He knew full well she didn't know yet what her plans were. She raised her chin. 'I think that is something I should discuss with Joe McQueen, not with you,' she said brusquely. 'I'll just unpack and change, and then I'll go and find him.'

'Get Elsie to take you to Mungo's study first,' Blade commanded with that air of arrogant authority that so exasperated her. 'I'll be there with Mary Lou. The study is also the general office. After I've introduced you to Mary Lou, I'll take you to see Joe.'

'I can find my own——' she began, but he was gone. *The General has issued his commands*, she thought facetiously, fighting down a wave of resentment at the way he was taking charge of her every action, even here at Windarra.

Keep your cool, Kelly, my girl, let him have his way—this time. Look on it as a neighbourly act. Your turn will come.

She saw that Elsie Duncan was busying herself making up the bed with fresh sheets.

'I'll finish that, Elsie. I'm sure you have plenty of other things to do.'

The woman straightened, eyeing her uncertainly. 'I'll

help you unpack,' she mumbled, tight-lipped and unsmiling.

'I can manage,' Kelly said pleasantly. She could read the woman loud and clear. Elsie didn't want to be openly rude in case Kelly decided to stay, but the housekeeper had no intention of making Windarra's new owner feel welcome either. Kelly wondered why. Had Blade Ryan succeeded in getting them all behind him already, all wound round his grasping little finger? She wouldn't put it past him. It was unlikely he would have hidden the fact that he wanted to own and run Windarra himself. He had been quick enough to tell *her*! It was plain that Elsie, despite her apparent awe of Blade Ryan, respected and approved of him—maybe even liked him as well. Mary Lou and Joe McQueen no doubt felt the same.

Elsie stood hesitating by the bed.

'I can manage, Elsie,' Kelly repeated. 'Thank you for offering.'

'Blade said—Mr Ryan said——' Elsie shifted awkwardly from one foot to the other.

'I'll find my own way to the study, thanks, Elsie. You go. I'll be fine.' Kelly bent dismissively over the nearest of her two suitcases. A moment later she heard Elsie shuffling out with a gruff, 'I'll be in the kitchen if you want me.'

As she rummaged in her case for a pair of jeans and a shirt, Kelly yawned. Only then did she realise how tired she was. Jet-lag, of course. The hot shower at Blade's apartment had helped, but its effects were wearing off now. She would have loved to crawl into bed right there and then, but she had learned, through years of travelling around the world, to resist the impulse to give in, and to adapt immediately to the hours of whichever new country she happened to be in.

Without pausing even to wash her face, she wriggled out of her blue knit dress into a pair of stretch jeans and a checked cotton shirt. After rolling up the sleeves and changing her shoes, she headed for the stairs. There was no sign of Elsie when she reached the lower level. She let her breath puff out in relief. Instead of heading for the living-area where she guessed her father's study—the office—

would be, she slipped out of the house by a side door.

A neat gravel path, lined with a low clipped privet hedge, led away from the house in the direction of the stables. She knew Blade Ryan would be angry—and perhaps Mary Lou, Windarra Stud's secretary, would feel slighted and hurt at being bypassed for now—but she wanted to seek out Joe McQueen and make herself known to him free of Blade Ryan's autocratic presence.

She came to a group of sheds and glanced inside. Tackrooms. A fly buzzed around her nose as she hurried on, past a holding-yard where a number of deep-bellied mares were awaiting the birth of their foals.

'Don't touch the fence—it'll give you a shock,' warned a voice.

She swung round to see a young man in khaki overalls emerging from one of the sheds with a bucket in each hand.

'Who are you?' He stopped dead, his pale blue eyes blinking at her under the slouch hat he wore at a jaunty angle. Suddenly a slow flush suffused his face. 'You're not——'

'Kelly Nagle Heath,' Kelly answered coolly, extending a hand. 'You're——?'

He lowered the buckets with a clatter. 'Name's Harry Watts, Miss—um—um——' It was clear he didn't know whether to call her Miss Nagle or Miss Heath.

'Kelly will be fine. Happy to meet you, Harry. I'm looking for Joe. Have you seen him?'

Harry's pale eyes, shaded by his broad-brimmed hat, appeared to be guardedly assessing her. As a woman? Or as his new boss?

'Joe went off to the house about ten minutes ago. Wonder you didn't see him on the way.'

To the *house*! She must have just missed him. Damn! How to outsmart yourself in one easy lesson. Joe was bound to be with Blade Ryan and Mary Lou by now, waiting for her to join them. She would have to go tamely back, cap in hand, and admit that she had disregarded Blade's request to come to the study first. It had been more like an order, but he would deny that of course. She would be made to feel like a recalcitrant schoolgirl. Unless . . .

Unless she could manage to slip back into the house without any of them realising she had left in the first place!

'Thanks, Harry.' She spun on her heel and hurried away, breaking into a run the moment she was out of sight.

'What's your hurry?' drawled an amused voice as she hurtled round a curve in the path, past a huge camellia bush covered with delicate pale pink flowers, straight into the arms of——

'Blade!' She tried to untangle herself as his arms closed involuntarily around her, her face flooding with colour, as much at his proximity as at being caught out.

'Goodness, my dear, what's wrong? Have you seen a ghost?'

His bantering tone dimly penetrated her scattered wits. She was pricklingly conscious of his hands still gripping her arms, the tips of his fingers acting like electric charges on her bare flesh.

It was ridiculous! She had never reacted this way before with any man. Even in Harvey Quinn's arms, she had never felt this alarming, paralysing weakness. She had always been in full control of her emotions—and her actions.

It was the jet-lag that was doing it, of course. In her weakened state, she simply wasn't herself; she had allowed Blade Ryan to get under her skin. So much so that now, caught like a rebellious child sneaking home after a forbidden jaunt, she had turned momentarily to water!

Having explained away her debilitating response, she felt better able to fight it. With a tug she jerked herself free. She stood facing him, chin tilted proudly, years of dealing with men of the world giving her a return of her normal poise.

'You—you startled me, that's all. Jumping out of the bushes like that.' With luck, he hadn't even noticed her peculiar reaction. She hoped not! She mustn't allow him to see any weak spots in her armour. That would be fatal.

'I thought you were the one who jumped out at me,' he murmured with heavy irony. 'I saw you leave the house from the office window—just after Joe walked into the room, as a matter of fact. I came after you to let you know.'

There was no censure in his voice. Clever Blade Ryan, she thought, her lips twisting. He was far too smart to make the mistake of chastising her for not following his instructions. He knew full well she would have a ready come-back to that one: *Why should I obey you? I'm the owner here, Blade Ryan, not you.*

'Joe's waiting inside for you.'

She realised that Blade had not fallen into step beside her, but was veering away in the direction of the drive where he had left his car. Had he intended all along to leave as soon as he had handed her over to Joe and Mary Lou? She felt a prickle of shame at her behaviour, which now seemed childish and pointless.

If Blade thought so too, he made no attempt to rub it in. How diabolically clever the man was!

'I must get back to Bilba.' He paused a moment, the late afternoon sun burnishing his hair as it lifted and fell with a breeze. 'I told Joe I'd come back in the morning and show you over the stud; he'll be tied up in the breeding-barn.' As she opened her mouth to declare that she could find her own way around the stud without his help, he forestalled her with a sardonic, 'Joe asked me if I would. I was coming over anyway. One of your brood-mare owners is visiting in the morning, a difficult man at the best of times. He says he refuses to deal with a woman, and is threatening to take his mares away from Windarra and send them to us.'

Kelly bit back a concerned gasp. She eyed Blade suspiciously, 'I should think that's just what you'd want, isn't it? Is that why you want to be on hand? To make sure I don't win him over?'

The grey eyes glinted with anger. 'I'm no pirate, Kelly. I don't want to take any of Mungo's mares away from Windarra, unless I see that you can't cope.' Kelly bristled. The threat was there, loud and clear. 'I merely thought I could smooth things over for you.'

'Thank you,' she replied stiffly. Why should he want to help her? she wondered frowningly as he strode off. She

tapped her chin. It wasn't so hard to guess. Seeing himself as
Windarra Stud's future owner, it would be in his own best
interests to maintain the status quo, to keep the existing
owners happy.

She sighed. Well, that would work both ways. By
soothing the ruffled feathers of difficult owners, he was
helping *her* as much as himself.

If she could trust him . . .

Exhausted as she was when she finally flopped into her
queen-sized bed around ten o'clock that evening, her mind
was still buzzingly awake, preventing her from dropping
off to sleep for some time.

She had spent the rest of the afternoon with Joe and
Mary Lou, going over the stud documents and talking
business. Mary Lou was a petite feathery blonde who,
though she appeared to be a bright enough secretary, spent
much of the afternoon idly examining her long painted
fingernails, patting her hair into shape, and glancing out of
the window as if expecting someone more exciting than Joe
or Kelly to pass by. Blade Ryan? Kelly wondered. Was
Mary Lou hoping he would come back to Windarra before
she left for the day? Could Mary Lou be the reason Blade
Ryan had spent so much time in Mungo Heath's office
lately? Fluffy feminine blondes were likely to be just the
type to appeal to a male chauvinist like Blade Ryan!

Joe McQueen was a rather harder nut to crack. He had
recoiled quite noticeably when they first came face to face.

'You're *her* all over again,' he had muttered, and his
disapproval chilled Kelly. Did he still despise Rowena after
all these years? And was he going to despise her, Kelly, too,
simply because she looked like her mother?

She had answered rather sharply, 'I'm not my mother,
Joe. My father——' she stressed the relationship '—was
aware of that when he left Windarra Stud to me. My
mother wasn't cut out for this kind of life. She missed her
old life and her acting too much. I'm different,' she said
with an intensity that kept Joe grudgingly intent on every
word. 'I've loved and worked with horses all my life, and I

prefer country to city life. Hard work and long hours are second nature to me. So never make the mistake of thinking you're dealing with someone who knows or cares nothing about this business, or someone who's going to give in at the first sign of trouble.'

Joe's unusual caramel-coloured eyes had wavered as she finished. Her vehemence—perhaps her straight-talking too—had surprised him. Good. Now he would know he wasn't dealing with a spoilt little heiress who looked on her inheritance simply as a means of making a fast buck.

It wasn't all plain sailing, even then. Joe had demurred when she insisted that he and Mary Lou go through all the books and costs and stud documents with her, explaining every tax and charge, everything to do with the stud.

'You don't need to bother yourself with all this, Miss— uh, Miss Nagle.'

'Heath. I'm Kelly Heath now, Joe. But please call me Kelly. Yes, of course I must know how the stud is run and what the costs are. I want to know everything. I want to know who sends their mares here, what bloodstock we own, cattle included, whether all our yearlings are to be prepared for sale or if we intend to keep some for ourselves, a hundred and one things.'

Finally Joe asked straight out, 'You're not planning to stay here *permanently* are you, Miss—er, Kelly?'

She bristled, tempted to fling back, 'Why not?' But that would give Joe the chance to speak out, to voice aloud the doubts he obviously shared with Blade Ryan. At length she had answered cautiously, 'I'd like a few days, Joe, to make up my mind. Because when I do, I assure you my decision will be irrevocable. Whatever I decide, it will be what I perceive will be best for Windarra. Never forgetting,' she pointed out deliberately, 'that my father trusted me enough to give me the choice. *He* believed I could do it, and that means a lot to me.' She eyed Joe steadily. 'I understand my father thought highly of you, Joe. I'd like to be able to rely on you, the way my father was able to.'

She put enough of a threat into her voice to make her meaning plain. Joe merely nodded, but she could see that

her words had given him something to think about. He
made no mention of Blade Ryan's offer to buy Windarra,
which rather surprised her. He must have been aware of it,
must have realised that Blade would already have
mentioned it to her. Joe's own silence on the subject was
significant—and heartening. It was imperative that she
gained Joe's trust as quickly as possible—and his respect.
She would need it if she stayed. Fighting Blade Ryan alone
would be like fighting an army single-handed. She would
need a few troops behind her.

When Mary Lou left at five o'clock, and Joe rose to leave
too, Kelly motioned him back.

'I'd like you to have dinner with me tonight, Joe,' she
said, deliberately making it more an order than a request so
that he wouldn't feel in a position to refuse. She wasn't sure
enough of him yet, and she wanted to keep the
upper hand—and for him to know that she held it. 'I'll go
and see Elsie now and arrange it. I want to know all about
the staff before I meet them tomorrow.'

Joe hesitated. 'I'll have to go and check on things in the
stables after dinner. It's my job to see that the lads have
done their work properly.'

'I won't keep you, Joe,' she promised. She had things she
wanted to do herself—things best done in the quiet of
evening. She wanted to spend some time in Mungo Heath's
library, absorbing information from his stud-books and
magazines.

Joe had rather self-consciously joined her at Mungo
Heath's heavy oak dining-table for a casserole dinner
prepared by Elsie Duncan, during the course of which he
gave her some valuable tips about the staff and their duties
and living-arrangements. Some of the staff lived in cottages
in the valley, others shared dormitory-style accommoda-
tion, while the rest travelled in daily, as Mary Lou did,
from outlying towns.

While they were on the subject of Mary Lou, Kelly took
the opportunity to ask casually, 'Does Mary Lou have a
special man in her life, Joe?' She was entitled to know, she
told herself. Especially if the man was Blade Ryan, who

wanted to take Windarra Stud from her!

'I wouldn't know anything about that, miss,' Joe had said, rather too quickly. He appeared to be avoiding her eye. Because he knew something he didn't want *her* to know? Or was it simply that he didn't believe in idle gossip? She had merely nodded, and left it there.

After dinner Joe had excused himself and hastened off, and after offering to help Elsie with the clearing up, and being refused with a sprightly, 'I can manage, thanks, it's what I'm paid for', Kelly retired to the library, and stayed there, poring over her father's magazines and books and newspaper clippings until her eyelids fluttered, refusing to stay open, and she dragged herself off to bed.

As she lay between the cool sheets, unable for a while to sleep, she tried to keep her mind off Blade Ryan by mulling over everything Joe had told her, and the helpful snippets of information she had picked up in the library.

But Blade Ryan was not a man who was easily dismissed, even from one's thoughts.

She had neatly, deliberately, steered the conversation at dinner away from Blade Ryan each time Joe McQueen brought up his name. She was anxious to lessen Blade Ryan's impact. She wanted Joe to know that Windarra Stud could run perfectly well without him, now that there was somebody else on hand who was equally capable of taking charge.

She sighed into her soft pillow. Did she honestly believe that she could do it? Deep, deep down, did she really believe that she could come all the way out here to Windarra Valley, Australia, and do as good a job as her father, with his lifelong experience in the breeding industry, or as good a job as Blade Ryan of Bilba? Mungo Heath and Blade Ryan were two tough, knowledgeable, powerful Australian *men*, while she . . .

She heaved another sigh. She had a feeling that Blade Ryan and Joe McQueen saw her merely as a spoilt young American show-jumper who naïvely thought she could succeed in any career she fancied, even the tough, competitive *man's* world of horse-breeding—until, like her mother, something better came along and she lost interest!

Damn it, *no*! Kelly punched the pillow with her fist. I will succeed. I'll show them what a woman—and a raw outsider—can do. See if I don't!

CHAPTER FOUR

IT WAS the touch of cool fingers on her bare shoulder that woke her next morning. Kelly's eyes flickered open.

Next moment she was sitting bolt upright in bed, her eyes snapping wide, suddenly unblinkingly awake.

'What are *you* doing in here?'

'Ah, so you're alive,' was Blade Ryan's complacent reply.

Colour flooded her cheeks as she realised her flimsy nightgown did little to conceal her naked curves. She grabbed the sheet and pulled it up to her chin.

'How *dare* you just walk into my bedroom?' Her eyes threw violet sparks. Who in the world did he think he was? Windarra Stud's master already? Even that would be no excuse! 'Without even knocking,' she fumed.

'I did knock,' Blade Ryan said calmly, not moving away from the bed; just standing there, looking from her vulnerable position, even taller and more of a threat than ever. 'I was having a cup of coffee downstairs while I was waiting for you to come down.' His eyes followed Kelly's as they flickered to her clock radio.

'I didn't expect you to be here so early,' she admitted defensively. 'I—I set my alarm, but it couldn't have gone off.'

'Oh, it went off all right.' Blade's tone was lazily amused. 'We could hear it from downstairs. When you didn't come down, Elsie started to get a bit worried. I offered to come up and investigate. When you didn't answer my knock I grew a trifle concerned myself.' He didn't *look* it, she thought, incensed. Faint scorn smouldered in his eyes. 'I thought I'd better take a look and make sure you were all right.'

'I could have been down in the stables,' Kelly argued, feeling at a distinct disadvantage with Blade Ryan towering, fully dressed, over her. She felt cornered and vulnerable and helpless—and she hated that—and *him*.

'I knew you weren't. I'd just come from there. Anyway, Elsie said you hadn't come down yet.'

'So you just walked straight in.' She tried to look outraged, but it wasn't easy, huddled half naked in bed with a sheet drawn up to her chin.

'I *looked* in first,' he defended himself mildly, his eyes glinting with arrogant mockery. 'I called your name—twice—but you didn't stir. I couldn't even see you breathing. Even if I had,' he admitted impenitently, 'it was time you woke up. We rise early on stud-farms, you know.'

She glared at him. 'Get out!' she snarled. 'I want to get dressed.'

'An excellent idea. I'll be waiting downstairs.' He swung away at last, and she felt her taut nerves relaxing. 'Don't go back to sleep,' he taunted over his shoulder as he headed for the door.

'I don't normally sleep in,' she hurled after him. 'And I don't normally sleep through alarms. I don't normally fly non-stop from Los Angeles to Sydney either and then bounce around in a light plane, all in the one day!'

He waved his hand in silent acknowledgement and disappeared through the doorway, leaving her sighing with frustration. Even though she had had the last word, she had the feeling that she had definitely come off second-best.

'Come and see your new foal,' Blade invited as they left the house together, having called an unspoken truce after she joined him downstairs for toast and coffee. Elsie wanted to cook her some breakfast, but she had declined, with profuse apologies for sleeping in.

'My new foal?' she echoed, frowning, faintly annoyed that Blade Ryan knew more about what went on at Windarra than she did. She knew she shouldn't feel that way—heavens, she'd only just arrived!—but she couldn't help it. She didn't like that gloating look in his eye or the barely masked cynicism in his voice. She suspected he was trying to deflate her—to seize every opportunity to belittle her—hoping to put her off her stride so that she would feel inadequate and unhappy and want to leave. So that she would sell up . . . to *him*.

'One of your mares gave birth this morning. Joe asked for my help when I arrived because the foal was pretty weak and having a minor breathing problem.' At Kelly's sharp look of concern, he was quick to reassure her. 'He's fine now. He and his mother are in one of the yearling boxes—I'd advise you to keep them there for a day or two, until the young fellow's a bit stronger.'

He led her past some buildings without stopping. 'Breeding-barn.' He waved a hand at one of the larger sheds. 'I'll show you inside later. The stables for the stallions are over there——' he inclined his head '—but they'll be out in their paddocks just now. We keep them out all morning—when they're not doing their duty in the breeding-barn.'

He didn't pause, hurrying her on. She had the impression he was anxious to show her around the stud in as short a time as decently possible—and then get rid of her. So that he could get on to real 'man's' work, no doubt, back home at his own stud! He had only offered to show her around to help Joe out, she must remember.

And—she jutted her chin—so that he could do his best to put her off the place at the same time!

Let him try, she thought rebelliously.

But she was forgetting the brood-mare owner who was going to call in later in the morning, the 'difficult' owner Blade had promised to pacify on her behalf. Blade couldn't leave, of course, until after he had been and gone.

'The owner who's coming . . .' She broached the subject in a brisk businesslike voice, quickening her steps to keep up with Blade's long stride. 'What time will he be here?'

'I told him to come around eleven o'clock.'

He had told him. Not Joe. How typical!

'They're in here,' Blade said, striding in ahead of her. The brightness of the morning sun was cut off abruptly as they passed through the open doorway of the yearling shed. The pungent smell of hay and horses, so well-loved and familiar, assailed Kelly's nostrils, sending shivers of delight down her spine. She followed Blade in silence, noting the rows of empty loose boxes on either side, until they reached the box where the new foal and its mother were recovering. Harry Watts, the pale-eyed young man who had met yesterday, was with them.

'He's only just on his feet,' Harry said after acknowledging Kelly's presence with a nod. He was looking at Blade, Kelly noted resentfully, not at her.

Blade inclined his head. 'Good. Thanks, Harry. I'll take over now.'

Harry didn't appear put out at being thus dismissed. With a brief salute, he ambled away.

'Take a look,' Blade invited, beckoning to Kelly.

She moved closer, peering into the box. 'Oh, isn't he adorable!' she cried involuntarily. 'A little chestnut.'

Wrinkle-nosed and warily alert, the foal, wobbling a little on its long awkward legs, threw back its head, still apprehensive about its brand new world. Its mother looked on—more uneasy, Kelly thought, than over-anxious.

Blade spoke in low soothing tones before opening the door and stepping inside. When he turned his head to speak to her, Kelly saw that he was frowning.

'The little chap's not suckling yet. I think they both need a bit of a hand.'

'Can I help?' she asked, and stood waiting tensely for a rebuff.

'You could hold the mare if you like. Thanks.' Blade was being thoroughly professional now, his veterinary instincts taking over. Any differences, any personal antagonisms between them were forgotten for now, the needs of the new foal uppermost in both their minds.

While she held the mare steady, Blade moved behind the foal and with the competence she was coming to expect from him, pressed his body against the little fellow's rump, one hand around the chest under the foal's neck, the other under the jaw, his fingers encircling the colt's fuzzy little chin. He urged the foal forward into the correct position, his body still braced against his rump. The foal struggled a moment, but with the help of Blade's guiding hand, the small muzzle found its target, and the next moment the foal was suckling contentedly, the mare looking equally at ease.

Kelly caught Blade's eye and a look passed between them, a look that transcended petty disagreements—or that was how she saw them in that moment. As petty and unnecessary.

Damn the man! She wished he had never told her that he wanted Windarra Stud for himself. She wished it wasn't too late for him to change his mind and withdrew the offer—and ease the pressure and the animosity and the resentment that his offer had brought with it. As a friend, as a close neighbour, and above all as a capable stud-master and veterinary surgeon, Blade Ryan would be an invaluable ally to call on in times of need. But how could she call on him under the present circumstances? She would only be playing into his hands, admitting that she couldn't cope!

'I'd better tell Harry all is well,' Blade said, waving her out of the box. 'I', not 'we', Kelly noted, her ire rising. Their truce—their moment of closeness—had been short-lived! 'After that I'll introduce you to the others,' Blade said brusquely, 'and then we'll go out into the paddocks.'

She controlled herself—just. It wasn't worth getting steamed up over trifles, when she could well have a full-scale battle on her hands before much longer. That was, if she decided to stay. She already had the strangest feeling that she had somehow come 'home', that this was where she was going to want to settle, once her surroundings became a little more familiar, and she had begun to find her feet.

Every instinct cried out to her that it was right, so very right, that *she* was the proper person to take over here . . . Not Blade Ryan, not any of the Ryans, and most certainly not a stranger. That would be unthinkable. She, Kelly Nagle Heath, was Mungo's rightful successor. And her father, in some miraculous way, had known it!

Realising her enthusiasm was carrying her away far too quickly, prematurely—she had barely seen anything yet, barely met anyone, barely *knew* anything—she consciously cast such thoughts aside—for now. But the excitement, the anticipation lingered, giving her a new peace of mind that

made her smile—openly—drawing a quizzical glance from
Blade Ryan.

She smiled more broadly then, tauntingly, nursing her
new contentment, the way a mischievous child hides
forbidden sweets. Let Blade Ryan lord it over her, just for
today. Once she knew her way around Windarra, once she
had met all the staff and was familiar with the procedures,
things would be different. She wouldn't need Blade Ryan's
constant presence, for one thing!

'Something amusing you? Or,' Blade's lip curled, 'are
you simply smiling at the thought of all your riches?
Owning all this . . . it must be heady stuff.'

She bit back the tart retort that sprang to her lips.
'Perhaps I'm just happy here,' she said shortly, lifting her
chin. She wasn't going to let him ruffle her.

His eyes narrowed as he looked into her face. 'I agree that
the miracle of a new life is a cause for happiness.' There was
a faint interrogation in his voice and, hearing it, her face
flamed in swift self-condemnation. Here she was, thinking
only of herself and of ridding Windarra of this man's
arrogant presence, while Blade Ryan was still thinking
solely of the new foal, of the miracle of life. She felt a rush of
shame.

'No?' His face hardened, the sneer on his lips making her
cringe inwardly. 'Of course . . . you would have been
thinking of all the lovely riches your new acquisition will
undoubtedly bring you in the years to come.' He stressed
the word 'acquisition', giving it a heartless, mercenary ring.
'He should fetch a good price. Assuming you sell him as a
yearling and don't decide to keep him for yourself—which
could of course prove equally profitable. He has the blood
of champions in his veins. Either way, you're in clover.
That is, unless——'

She broke in, snapping out each word to hide the
wretchedness she felt inside, 'You've already told me about
all the nasty pitfalls that can befall a young thoroughbred. I
don't need to be——'

'I'd keep them in mind, if I were you.' His voice grated
over hers. 'If financial gain is so dear to your heart, being

aware of what can happen to prevent all that lovely cash
rolling in will save you a lot of heartache later on, when
something actually does happen.'

She seethed with impotent rage, speechless at being so
misunderstood. Trying to defend herself now would only
make things worse, she decided with a stifled sigh, and,
tossing her dark head in exasperation, she began to walk
on.

'This way,' Blade rasped, and she had to suffer the
indignity of turning back and trotting after him as he
strode off in the opposite direction.

They managed to remain civil to each other for the
remainder of the morning, as Blade led her in and out of
ivy-covered stone buildings and galvanised-iron sheds,
describing their various functions and introducing her to
the staff. One of the buildings was Mungo Heath's well
equipped veterinary surgery.

'He was very proud of it,' Blade remarked. 'There's a
visiting vet in regular attendance, but you can feel free to
call on me too at any time.'

'Thank you,' Kelly said gratefully, wondering how long
his offer would stand.

They didn't stay in the stable complex for the whole
morning, Blade ushering her out into the white-railed
paddocks at one stage to mingle with the mares and foals.
The visiting mares were kept close to the stables, where it
was handy for their owners to inspect them, while the
Windarra-owned mares were paddocked further afield.
Blade, his veterinary instincts taking over, examined the
mares while she silently watched and absorbed. Smilingly,
she fondled the long-legged foals that gambolled alongside
their mothers, speaking in low, gentle tones to make herself
known to them and put them at their ease. She caught
Blade watching her once or twice, but he made no
comment.

Afterwards they wandered through the sweet-smelling
grasses of the yearling paddocks, where the young glossy-
coated colts and fillies, in their separate paddocks, brought

gasp after gasp of delight from Kelly.

'They're simply beautiful,' she breathed, misty-eyed with admiration.

'A promising bunch,' Blade Ryan agreed, standing ankle-deep in grass, his hands on his hips, squinting against the sun. He looked as much a part of the landscape, Kelly thought with a strange lump catching in her throat, as the grazing horses. They all seemed to belong, to be an integral part of this pure horse-country. Would she too belong here one day?

'Future champions, without a doubt.' Blade raised a cynical eyebrow. 'Worth their weight in gold,' he drawled, with a return of his former derision.

This time she let it wash over her, barely even tempted to utter a retort. It was hard to hold grudges out here, with the bright spring sunshine beating down on her head and the fresh, springy grass beneath her feet, while away in the hazy blue distance the timbered mountains thrust into the clear blue sky, wrapped over one another like benign, protective giants.

She breathed in deeply, gulping the fresh clean air into her lungs and exulting in a new sense of freedom; feeling her heart expanding and her skin tingling. No wonder her father had loved the valley so.

She had to shake herself to concentrate on what Blade was saying, his back to her now as he headed for the gate.

'We'd better head back,' he was saying. 'Our friend should be arriving shortly. We'll leave the breeding-barn and the stallions until later.'

She was surprised that the time had passed so quickly. With each passing minute she was finding her new world more fascinating, feeling its lure, its magic—and the thought excited her. Her father had felt that same magic, and he had left Windarra Stud to her so that she might feel it too.

Might feel it . . . and want to stay here and run the place herself? Had that been her father's secret wish?

Just as they reached the stable yard, they heard tyres crunching on the gravel drive. As a late-model Mercedes swung into the yard, Kelly swallowed nervously. How was she going to convince this 'difficult' owner who 'didn't like dealing with women' that his mares would not be disadvantaged by the change in ownership?

A massive balding man wearing a sports jacket and a loud bow tie heaved himself out of the car. Kelly didn't wait for Blade to introduce her. It was a moment to assert her authority, she decided, marching forward, hand outstretched.

'Mr Carter? I'm Kelly Nagle Heath. I'm happy to tell you that your new foal is doing just fine.' She had earlier learned from Blade which mare belonged to Sam Carter, and had taken special note of the mare's pretty two-day-old filly. 'Would you like to have a look at the filly now, or would you rather wait until after lunch? You *will* stay to lunch?' She had thought to warn Elsie earlier of possible guests for the midday meal.

She sensed that she had rather taken the wind out of the sails of her visitor, and out of Blade Ryan too, she suspected with some gratification—he hadn't said a single word so far.

'Thank you,' Sam Carter said gruffly. 'Kind of you—though I'd like to see the filly first.'

'By all means.' She turned to Blade Ryan. 'Do you wish to come with us, Blade? I'd appreciate it if you would. I've only just arrived from the States,' she explained unnecessarily to Sam Carter—as if he wouldn't know!—'and you may have some questions that Blade could answer more readily than I would be able to just yet. Or you could speak to Joe McQueen if you'd prefer. I want you to know,' she added in cool, clipped tones, 'that all the mares and foals entrusted to Windarra Stud will be cared for exactly as they were when my father was here.'

Her visitor eyed her warily through his rimless spectacles. 'But you've had no experience in this business, have you, Miss Nagle?'

Kelly answered swiftly, before Blade Ryan could put in a word for her, as he seemed about to do. She sensed that if she allowed him to step in and defend her, it could ring false; it

could weaken her in Sam Carter's eyes, and end up going
against her. 'Mr Carter—my name is Heath now, Kelly
Nagle Heath. I have worked with thoroughbreds nearly all
my life,' she added crisply, giving neither of them a chance
to speak, 'and I have always been considered extremely
capable. Capable and strong and very determined. My
father knew of my successes in the show-jumping field, and
how dedicated I was to a life with horses, and I know he
would never have left Windarra Stud to me had he had any
doubts about my ability to run the stud as successfully as he
managed to.' That was aimed at Blade Ryan, though she
didn't look at him.

'You mean—you're thinking of staying and running
Windarra Stud *yourself*?' Her visitor's florid face showed his
astonishment. 'But we've all been expecting you to sell up!
Or at least to put a manager in charge while you go back to
your show-jumping career in America.'

Kelly felt a wave of rebellion. First Blade Ryan, now
Sam Carter! Couldn't these men get it into their heads that
a woman was every bit as capable as a man of running a
thoroughbred horse-stud—*and* sticking it out, even through
the bad times! She had proved she was as good as any man
in the show-jumping arena—why not in the thoroughbred-
breeding business as well?

'Would it be so unthinkable, Mr Carter?' she challenged
coolly. Even though it was far too early—even though she
knew she needed more time before finally and irrevocably
making up her mind—it wouldn't hurt to let them both
think she had already decided to stay. It certainly wouldn't
hurt to let Blade Ryan think so!

Sam Carter gaped at her. 'Why would a pretty young
girl like you—one of your country's top show-jumpers—
want to stay out here in Australia doing back-breaking,
heart-breaking work like this?'

Again Kelly avoided looking at Blade Ryan, who was
being ominously silent.

'I was a show-jumper for a long time, Mr Carter,' she
said, curbing her rising anger. As before, her words were
intended for Blade Ryan. 'You can grow tired of being in

the limelight—tired of the incessant travelling—tired of performing in one narrow field for too long. And now that I've lost my beloved mare Pixie, I've lost what little enthusiasm I still had for show-jumping. We were a team for so long. I feel I need a new challenge now—something quite different. So long as it's with horses.'

'But—but Windarra Valley's so far from your home!' Sam Carter spluttered.

She threw back her head, assuring him—and Blade Ryan—'I already feel at home in Windarra Valley, Mr Carter. As if I belong here. I feel I have an *obligation* to stay, for my father's sake.'

She glanced at Blade Ryan at last to see how he was taking all this, but his face was a coldly impassive mask. If he was angry with her, he was containing it well.

'I'm keen to see that nothing changes here at Windarra Stud, now that my father's no longer here,' she told Sam Carter for the second time, aware as she spoke of a stir of excitement deep within her. 'If I'm here, I can make *sure* that nothing changes.'

She paused, gathering her strength, knowing she would need it now that she had virtually thrown down the gauntlet at Blade Ryan's aggressive feet. If he thought she had already made up her mind to stay, would it keep him off her back? Or would he still try to change her mind, still find obstacles to put in her path, still hope that she would ultimately fail to make a go of it?

Well, Blade Ryan, she thought spiritedly, do your darnedest! I'll sink or swim entirely on my own merits—or failings! And *if* I fail, it won't be through any goading or interference from you! But I'll succeed. I'll succeed *despite* your efforts to stop me!

Blade Ryan had said nothing all this time. But she knew he would be thinking plenty! She had a feeling that the moment their visitor left he would pour out precisely what he thought of her impetuous announcement. He would call it gross stupidity, no doubt, or even spite, or the mindless whim of a spoilt, rebellious female who didn't know what she was letting herself in for. He would equate her with her mother, who had given up a glamorous career of her own to marry Mungo Heath and live in outback Australia—only to run away three years later, bored out of her mind!

Let him think as he pleased! She would make up her own mind in her own good time, and in the meantime let him think she was definitely staying. Let him get used to the idea that Windarra had a new owner—that Windarra was not going to fall into his lap simply because *he* wanted it to happen.

Smilingly, she took Sam Carter's arm, steering him towards the paddock where his mare and new foal were enjoying the sunshine.

A decidedly mollified Sam Carter drove off in a cloud of dust after lunching on the veranda with Kelly and Blade. Now, with their visitor gone, Kelly found herself alone with Blade Ryan, in the shade of the same gum tree she had plucked a leaf from when she first arrived.

Blade surprised her by making no reference to her rash announcement earlier than she intended to stay. None at all.

'We could go and see the stallions now,' was all he said. Businesslike, autocratic, his face impassive. 'Breeding-barn first.' He turned to go.

Contrarily, because he was avoiding the issue, she decided to bring it up herself, to find out precisely where she stood—and in particular what she was up against.

She caught up with him. 'I thought you might want to withdraw your offer to show me around, now that I've told you I won't be selling Windarra.'

His steps slowed. He looked down at her, a cynical eyebrow shooting upward. 'A woman can always change her mind,' he said insolently.

She bit back a gasp. 'Are you going to show me around or not?' she snapped.

A ray of sunlight pierced the branches above them, catching him in the eye, intensifying the startling grey. He demanded curtly, 'Why should I break a promise to Joe simply because you've made an announcement that's not in my favour? Do you think I'm that small-minded? Come on, let's go.'

He was telling her that he was showing her around merely as a favour to Joe, that his opinion of her didn't enter into it.

He didn't wait for her answer, and she had none to offer—not aloud, at any rate. No, Blade Ryan, she thought in grudging admiration, I don't think you are small-minded at all. Far from it. Dangerous, cunning, shrewd as a fox, but small-minded you most certainly are not. Blade Ryan, she was beginning to realise, a coil of anxiety tightening inside her, was a force to be reckoned with—and that bothered her. She, Kelly Nagle Heath, so accustomed to holding all the cards where men were concerned, was unsure of her hand this time. It was the one shadow on an otherwise sunny horizon.

Inside the spacious breeding-barn, Joe was too busy even to acknowledge their presence when they slipped into a corner to watch proceedings. Harry Watts was there, Kelly noticed, holding a bay mare while Joe and a muscular young man with thick black hair and bold dark eyes, called Nico, were guiding a magnificent black stallion into position.

'It's Kinman,' Blade whispered. 'A high-spirited fellow—hasn't been here long. You never know quite what to expect from him.'

There was much grunting going on, interspersed with sharply spoken commands from Joe and Nico, who obviously needed all their strength to hold and manoeuvre the big stallion.

Kelly stood watching in respectful silence, well aware that stallions had a reputation for wildness and for being difficult to handle—this one, plainly, more than most. The saying 'strong as a horse' seemed particularly apt in Kinman's case!

Conscious of a sidelong glance from Blade Ryan, she kept her features composed. Was he expecting her to show fear?

Embarrassment? Dismay? Dismay at finding out that
breeding thoroughbreds was no exercise for the weak or the
faint-hearted? She could almost hear him taunting her:
*Can't you see that because of the strength involved here, this is a man's
job rather than a woman's?*

When it was over, Blade led her into the adjoining
laboratory to explain briefly a few of the procedures
involved and the necessity for keeping samples and records.
A few minutes later they emerged from the building,
blinking in the harsh sunlight.

'Now you can meet the other stallions,' Blade decided in
his peremptory way, and again she was conscious of a
sidelong glance. Was he hoping to detect some reluctance in
her? Hoping that she might have had enough of headstrong
stallions for one day? Or for ever, perhaps? Maybe he was
hoping she would be ignorant enough to approach them too
quickly and get kicked in the head!

Joe McQueen was coming out of one of the stallion-boxes
as they approached.

'Be wary of Kinman if you go in,' he advised gruffly.
'I've just brought him back and he's still a bit frisky.'

'We will,' Kelly said with a quick smile, saying 'we'
deliberately to include Blade Ryan. Why shouldn't he be as
careful as she? Or had her pushy neighbour from Bilba
come to know the Windarra stallions so intimately in these
past weeks that he could approach them with impunity?

All five stallions were fine-looking, glossy-coated ani-
mals with, as she was well aware, the blood of champions
coursing through their veins. She kept at a sensible
distance, treating them with the respect they deserved—
particularly the fiery Kinman. The exception was Rey-
burn, a fine long-necked chestnut who, less wary than the
others, stood calmly while she patted him, Blade holding
him steady, just in case.

'Superb, aren't they?' Blade said generously, his admiration overcoming for now the hostility between them.
'Windarra stallions have produced winners of all the
principal races in Australia. We have the same record at
Bilba, except for one race.' His tone changed palpably.

'The Melbourne Cup. We've never managed to win the big one.'

The Melbourne Cup . . . Australia's richest, most famous race! Kelly saw something kindle in Blade's grey eyes.

'We're hoping to win it this year though, with our horse Sherwin,' he added frankly. 'He's won a string of races so far—some of our best—but this is the one we want.' He ushered her out, locking the door behind him. 'Here, you'd better have these.' He tossed her the keys. 'They were Mungo's. Joe has a set of his own.'

'Thank you,' she said politely, pocketing them. So Blade Ryan had had her father's keys. No doubt he had been hoping to keep them! Now, in view of her announcement that she intended to stay, he knew he must give them up. But had he also given up his ambition to own Windarra some time in the future?

Hardly! He had already hinted that he expected her to change her mind about staying. If she knew Blade Ryan, he would already be secretly plotting ways to undermine her confidence and turn her decision around!

Blade's voice, quietly laconic, broke into her thoughts. 'Heathcote could win it, of course.'

'Heathcote? My father's horse?' She felt a leap of excitement. 'You mean he's running in the Melbourne Cup too?'

'Yes, didn't Joe mention it? Your father intended retiring Heathcote to stud at the end of this spring season—after running him in the Melbourne Cup. Whether he wins or not, his stud career looks rosy. He has impeccable blood-lines, and he's already a Derby winner—and he's had plenty of other good wins. But Mungo felt that a Melbourne Cup win would be an added feather in his cap—a fitting swan-song. Naturally, we think our Sherwin has an equally good chance.'

She looked at him quickly. 'Then you *were* rivals—you and my father,' she accused.

'I never denied that. But I said it was a *friendly* rivalry. It never interfered with out basic friendship.'

And now? Kelly's teeth tugged at her lip. Now that her

father was gone, would there still be friendly rivalry between the two stud-farms? Would there still be friendship?

She almost laughed aloud. How could there be?

'They're competing against each other this coming weekend, as a matter of fact,' Blade said as they headed back to the house. 'It's the Caulfield Cup on Saturday, the first leg of the big spring carnival. I'll be flying down to Melbourne for the race. If you decide you can spare the time to go, you can fly down with me.'

'Thank you,' she said non-committally. If only she could fly a plane herself! She could be independent of this man! She couldn't ask Joe to fly her down—he was far too busy just now.

'Winning the Caulfield Cup and the Melbourne Cup in the same year is considered quite a coup,' Blade added. 'And either of our horses could do it. Heathcote or Sherwin.'

She didn't like the mocking gleam in his eyes. Was he deliberately trying to underline the rivalry between them? To underline that she was not her father, or anything like his friend Mungo Heath, that the 'friendly rivalry' between Windarra and Bilba was now a thing of the past?

It would be unfortunate, even sad, if that were true, she reflected with a sigh; but in view of Blade Ryan's ruthless ambition to get his hands on Windarra, how could it be otherwise?

'Thank you for your help today,' she said with studied politeness when they came within sight of the house. Blade's Land Rover stood in the shade of the tall gum tree. 'I'd better go in and see if there have been any calls for me, and I want to go through a few things with Mary Lou.' She spoke dismissively, maintaining her polite tone. 'I guess you're anxious to get back to Bilba, you've wasted nearly a whole day running around after me.'

'I don't consider it a waste,' he said with an enigmatic smile—just enough of a smile to set her nerve-ends tingling with the memory of other, more spontaneous smiles, and the way she had reacted to them.

'My mother would like you to come to dinner tomorrow night,' he added, halting near the steps, his thumbs thrust aggressively into the pockets of his thigh-hugging jeans.

She looked up at him in surprise—and felt something catch in her throat. The sunlight was striking Blade's tawny hair from behind, turning the fine strands on top to shining gold. For a brief, insane moment, she had the wildest, stupidest impulse to reach up and run her fingers through its gilded smoothness, imagining idly that it would feel rather like trickling one's fingers through the soft warm sands of Santa Monica beach.

She realised uneasily that she had never once thought of running her fingers through Harvey Quinn's wild, dark hair, and she mentally shook herself, bitter with self-condemnation. She must still be suffering from jet-lag, to sink to this level, to have absurd, unwanted fantasies about the very man she should be most on her guard against!

'My sister Megan will be home for the evening,' Blade remarked, seemingly unaware of the chaotic turn of her thoughts. 'And Dan Cassidy, Megan's fiancé, will be there too, of course. Will you come?' he asked abruptly—so abruptly that she had the feeling he was expecting her to refuse. Or hoping she would?

She lifted her chin. 'I'd love to come.' She was anxious to meet Blade Ryan's family, her nearest neighbours; anxious to meet his mother in particular—Grace Ryan, who had known both Mungo Heath and her mother during the happier days of their marriage. Kelly wondered why Grace Ryan appeared so anxious to meet *her*. Was she merely curious to see if the daughter had turned out to be like the mother? She already knew they looked alike, she had seen those magazine photographs. Or was it simply a neighbourly gesture—the polite thing to do? Kelly hoped it was more than that, that Blade's mother was extending her hand in genuine friendship. The very fact that Grace Ryan was inviting her to dinner, not simply to call in for a drink or for afternoon tea, seemed to indicate that it wasn't a mere token gesture, that she was willing to meet her half-way. *More* than half-way.

'Good.' Blade swung away. 'I'll come and pick you up at six.' He didn't wait to see if that suited her. No. Kelly tightened her lips. Blade Ryan wouldn't. He was so accustomed to calling all the shots, to having others fall in with his every wish, his every command. Well, Blade Ryan, she thought, throwing back her head in defiance, resisting the temptation to glare after him, knowing she might be tempted instead to follow the line of his broad shoulders and the easy swinging motion of his hips, I can afford to let you have your way on these small issues. It is the larger ones you will find difficult to win!

She marched up the steps into the house.

She spent the rest of the afternoon with Mary Lou in the office, and the evening in her father's library. She made sure the next morning that she didn't sleep in, rising early to go down to the stables to give a hand wherever it was most needed. The young stable-hands treated her with caution until they realised that she knew as much about horses as they did, and in some cases more. She managed to catch a few brief moments now and again with Joe McQueen, and spent the rest of the day back at the house, returning phone-calls, examining correspondence and studying records. She also put a call through to her mother in Los Angeles, steeling herself first for Rowena's reaction to the news that she was thinking seriously of keeping Windarra Stud and running the place herself, and had decided to stay on for a while to find out for sure.

When the expected explosion came, she barely flinched.

'You and Chuck can come out for Christmas, if I do stay,' she soothed. 'If you can't get away, I'll try to fly home.'

'There, you see?' Rowena pounced on the word. 'You still think of Los Angeles as "home"! Darling, don't do anything hasty. Think carefully before you commit yourself. If you should fail . . .'

'I don't intend to fail, Mother.'

'No, darling, of course you don't *intend* to fail, but if you *do*—through no fault of your own—just think what it would mean. You'd have a liability on your hands. You could end up with nothing . . . ruined!'

'Thanks for the vote of confidence,' Kelly said drily. 'I'm willing to take that chance, Mother. But I happen to think I *can* make a go of it.'

'Well, darling,' Rowena's sigh came through the line, saying even more loudly than words precisely what she was thinking, 'at least you know you'll always have your show-jumping to go back to. If necessary, we'd help you out the way we did when——'

'Mother, I won't be going back to show-jumping. Whatever happens. How's Chuck?'

'He's fine. He'll be as anxious as I am about this——' she curbed herself '—about what's in your mind. Oh, God, if Mungo Heath ever wanted revenge, he's certainly succeeded hands down. He must be laughing in his grave!'

'Mother, from what I've learned about my father,' she stressed the relationship, 'that last thing he ever wanted was revenge. He loved you—he never got over losing you.'

Rowena's harsh laugh crackled over the line. 'Who told you that fairy-tale? He *hated* me—and Chuck too—and even you, darling, meant nothing to him—he never even wanted to see you. If you had heard the cruel things he said to me the day I left Windarra——'

'He was lashing out in anger to cover his *hurt*, Mother. Surely you must have realised that? You had just told him you loved another man and that you wanted to go back to the States and marry him—and in the same breath you told him the man you now loved would be bringing up *his* child! How did you expect him to react?'

'In a far more civilised fashion,' Rowena snapped, but Kelly sensed that her mother's outrage rose largely from a sense of guilt. Aware of that, she didn't pursue the subject, switching instead to more practical matters.

'Mother, there are a few things I'd like to have sent out here. The rest can come later—if I decide to stay permanently. Do you have a pencil?'

She ran through her list of requirements, ending the call with the excuse that she had to rush and get ready for her visit to Bilba Stud. Rowena sounded surprised, and was unable to resist the comment that Grace Ryan always did do the 'right thing', whether she wanted to or not, when Kelly told her about her invitation to dinner. The long-suffering note in Rowena's voice lingered as she bid Kelly goodbye.

The moment Kelly replaced the receiver, breathing a sigh of relief that the call was behind her, the phone shrilled beneath her fingers. Picking it up again, she said, 'Windarra Stud. Kelly Heath speaking.'

'Blade here.'

Her heart gave a tiny jump. What was Blade doing phoning at this hour? His voice sounded curt, even grim; it was obviously not a social call. Had he thought of a way to dissuade her from staying, and couldn't wait until next day to inject his poison?

She started to mouth a cautious 'Yes?' but he didn't wait to hear it.

'Mother's had a bad fall. I'm flying her down to Sydney for treatment. Megan's going with us.'

'Oh, Blade, I hope she's not badly——'

'Megan thinks her wrist is broken,' Blade cut in. 'She jarred herself badly as well, trying to protect her bad hip when she fell. We think it's best to take her to her own specialist in Sydney rather than the bush hospital where Megan works.'

'I hope she's not in too much p——'

'Megan's making her as comfortable as she can for the trip. Afraid the dinner tonight is off.'

'Oh don't worry about——'

'Have to go. Sorry about tonight.' The line went dead.

Kelly felt a vague sense of disappointment. She had been looking forward to meeting Grace Ryan, and Megan and Megan's fiancé Dan Cassidy as well. She hoped Grace's wrist was not badly broken and that her fall had not caused any additional damage to her arthritic hip.

With a long free evening now stretching ahead, she returned to the stables to accompany Joe on his rounds, and after returning to the house to cook herself an omelette for dinner, for she had sent Elsie Duncan home early, thinking she would be out for the evening, she retired to the library to bury herself in her father's books.

CHAPTER FIVE

When Kelly telephoned Bilba next morning to enquire about Grace Ryan, Dan Cassidy, Megan Ryan's fiancé, answered the phone.

'They're keeping her in hospital for one more night,' Dan told her. He spoke in an easy-going drawl, with no hint of the derision and the hostility that was so often evident in Blade Ryan's voice. 'Her wrist's been put in plaster. Luckily, it's not a serious break. But she's hurt her hip as well, and they want to keep her under observation for another day before they let her come home. Megan and Blade intend flying home later this morning. Megan wants to go back to her own hospital and arrange some time off to look after Grace, and Blade wants to catch up on a few things here.'

Kelly wondered at the lack of resentment in Dan's voice. He didn't sound a bit put out that Blade Ryan needed to 'catch up on things' at Bilba, even though Dan must know that it was owing to Blade spending so much of his time lately at Windarra Stud, and even though it must have meant an extra work-load on Dan's own shoulders. But then, hadn't Blade said that Dan Cassidy was keen to run Bilba himself? Most likely Dan was relishing his extra responsibilities, and hoping that Blade's campaign to get his hands on Windarra would succeed, since it would be advantageous to both.

'Let me know it there's anything I can do,' she offered, stifling her speculation with a hidden sigh.

'Thanks. We're all sorry about last night,' Dan said affably.

Were they? wondered Kelly as the insidious doubts crept back, the doubts her mother had put there. 'Grace Ryan always does the right thing, whether she wants to or not,' Rowena had said on the phone. A subtle dampener, aimed at discouraging her—not unlike Blade Ryan's own attempts, Kelly thought with an upsurge of rebellion. Well, she was not going to let either of them undermine her confidence. Resolutely, she cast her doubts aside.

'I was sorry too,' she said, adding lightly, 'not to worry, there'll be plenty of time later on. I guess Blade's told you I've decided to stay on here.' Dan Cassidy might as well be prepared too.

'You have?' He sounded surprised.

'You mean he didn't tell you?' she inquired silkily, adding with a short laugh, 'I have a feeling he doesn't believe it yet—or *want* to believe it.'

Dan muttered something unintelligible, and Kelly took pity on the amiable studman, whose embarrassment suggested a gentle nature, far more amiable and conciliatory than that of his predatory future brother-in-law. Swinging the conversation back to Grace Ryan, she said, 'Please send Mrs Ryan my best wishes for a speedy recovery.'

'I will. Thanks for calling.'

Kelly worked hard for the rest of the day, spreading her time between the office and the stables. With each passing hour she was gaining confidence, feeling more at home, and liking her new life even more than she had imagined she could.

It was tiring though. She found she was looking forward to a soaking bath and a quiet evening in her father's library with her feet up and the soothing strains of Mozart or Beethoven playing in the background. She recalled with a faint sigh that she had asked Harry Watts, who was on duty in the stables tonight, to call her if any of the imminent foals arrived in the night. She wanted to be there, even if he didn't require her help. A sudden smile overtook her sigh. Exhausted as she was, she knew that the sight of a healthy new-born foal would quickly wash away her weariness and fill her with a sense of exultation instead.

Late in the afternoon she headed back to the house, wanting to catch Mary Lou before she left for the day, to check if there had been any urgent messages. Walking, head bowed in thought, she jumped as a shadow fell across the privet-lined path ahead. Looking up, she saw a tall masculine figure blocking her path. Her heart did a double flip.

'Blade!' She frowned slightly—at herself rather than at him. Why should her heart leap at the sight of this man, when it should quail instead? Blade Ryan meant nothing but trouble!

'You look tired,' he said, observing her through half-closed lids. Hiding the satisfaction he felt? she wondered, piqued. Did he think she was ready to quit already, simply because her limbs felt a bit weary and her eyelids a trifle heavy? If so, he didn't know Kelly Nagle Heath! Many a time as a top international show-jumper she had felt almost too exhausted to continue, but she had always managed to shake off the feeling and go on. Her numerous successes had made it all worthwhile, pumping her with fresh adrenalin and renewing her in body and spirit. Only it had been more than merely winning that had kept her going, it had been the competition, the companionship, the communication between horse and rider . . . so many things.

And now she felt that same challenge, that same satisfaction, here at Windarra.

'I was thinking,' she snapped back, and regretted the sharpness in her voice when she saw Blade Ryan's lip twist contemptuously. Darn, she was sure *acting* as though she were tired! Tired and snappy and irritable. 'How is your mother?' she asked in a milder tone.

'Much better, thanks. I've just phoned the hospital and the jarring they were worried about doesn't appear to have done her any real harm. She can come home tomorrow; I'll fly down in the morning to pick her up. Megan's taking time off work to look after her.' Blade's eyes seemed to be giving her some kind of message. Chauvinist that he was, it wasn't hard to guess that it would be something along the lines of *a woman's place is in the home*! Blade Ryan obviously expected his womenfolk to put home and family first, work second. No, not second—most definitely a poor last!

'I'm glad your mother's going to be all right,' she said, curbing her mutinous feelings. Why couldn't Blade have told her all this on the phone? Why had he come to Windarra?

He must have read the question in her eyes. 'I've come to take you for a drive. To give you a break,' he said, and the unexpectedness of it left her momentarily speechless. *Blade Ryan*, being thoughtful and considerate? There had to be a catch!

'A break . . . where?' she asked cautiously, when she had recovered her power of speech.

'To the ghost-gum forest.' He swept a hand in the direction of the dimpled purple mountains. 'The forest is high up above the valley. It'll take a couple of hours. The forestry people are extending the forest-track up there. I'd like to take a look.'

Her interest stirred. But two whole hours . . . 'I was just going in to see if Mary Lou has any urgent——'

'She hasn't. I've just been in to see her. I thought you might have been in there with her,' he added as she looked at him sharply.

I'll bet, she thought, and at once felt a prickly of heat running along her cheek-bones. Startled, she thought: It can't be *jealousy*! Promptly—inwardly—she laughed the idea to scorn. She was feeling piqued, that was all. Mary Lou was *her* private secretary, not Blade Ryan's—and she resented Blade interfering.

'I'll have to let Elsie know,' she said briskly, to cover her reaction. She hoped he hadn't read her thoughts again! 'She'll be preparing my dinner.'

'I've already told Elsie. She's going to leave you something to heat up when you get back. Enough for two, she says.' His grey eyes mocked her. 'OK with you?'

She grimaced, 'I guess so.' He knew full well that if she had had a choice, she would never have invited him to stay for dinner!

'You'll need a jacket,' he said, swinging away, his arm brushing hers as he turned, the innocent contact causing a funny little tingle to run through her. Antipathy, not attraction, she asserted silently, with a quick frown.

'It'll be cool up there,' Blade tossed over his shoulder. 'Elsie's preparing a flask of hot soup for us. You can pick it up when you fetch your jacket.'

He had taken care of everything—as usual! And now he was telling her what to do. *Fetch your jacket, pick up the flask, do this, do that.* Kelly sighed, her spirit of independence struggling for a moment to disrupt his carefully-laid plans. But she couldn't for the life of her see any real reason why she *should* disrupt them without appearing petty, which she prided herself she was not.

'Give me five minutes,' she said, and hastened into the house before he could rasp 'Four!'—or 'Three!'—simply to assert his dominance over her.

The thought made her chuckle to herself—if ruefully. Honestly, Blade Ryan was making her thoroughly paranoid!

Emerging with a tan suede jacket slung over her shoulders and Elsie's flask of hot soup clasped in her hand, she saw that Blade was already seated behind the wheel of the Land Rover and realised irritably that he had the engine running. A subtle rebuke for being two minutes late? Typical, she thought. Blade Ryan being masterful to the end!

Unhurriedly she approached the vehicle and climbed into the passenger-seat beside him, making a show of dusting the seat first.

Leaving the homestead behind, they drove between the lush white-fenced paddocks until they began climbing the timbered slopes. On the higher ground, Saint Gertrudis cattle grazed contentedly in the orange glow of the late afternoon sun. The road soon became steep, needing Blade's full attention. Kelly sat back, the sights and sounds around her gradually soothing her frayed nerves. The mountain gums were alive with bell-birds, their distinctive tinkling call pricking the atmosphere. Surprise parties of wild parrots in bawdy cerise, gold, puce and paris green soared overhead, and audacious black-and-white magpies swooped on the intruding Land Rover. Kelly threw up a hand to protect herself when one irate magpie, frighteningly large at such close quarters, almost crashed through the glass windscreen.

'It's nesting time,' Blade remarked, looking unperturbed. 'They're not kindly disposed towards intruders.'

As they rose higher, the dirt road grew soft and dank from the moist forest floor. The air was cold and dark from the soaring columns of gums, aptly named ghosts. Smooth and pale-skinned, they rose in silent splendour hundreds of feet into the mountain air to branch in the far-up sun. There was no underbush, only the brown, furred stalks of monstrous tree ferns.

Blade rolled the car to a stop and turned off the engine.

'Let's walk,' he said and with a nod she climbed out. The fern mould made their feet absolutely soundless. The bell-birds could have been boy sopranos in a distant choir-stall.

'It's like a cathedral, soaring and silent,' Kelly murmured, clasping her hands almost reverently to her chest. 'And the bell-birds are the choirboys.'

Blade turned to look at her, watching in silence as she approached one of the slender ghost gums. She ran her hands over the silky smoothness of its trunk and found her palms covered with a smooth white powder.

She looked up at Blade and smiled. 'Thank you for bringing me here,' she said simply, forgetting for a moment the animosity between them. Her smile faded under his continued scrutiny. Something in his expression puzzled her. 'What is it?' she asked, frowning. Suddenly she felt distinctly uneasy.

'Your mother hated it up here,' Blade said at length. 'I thought you would have hated it too.'

His words, in the breath-taking stillness, jarred like the rasp of a chain-saw.

'Is that why you brought me up here?' she demanded, shaking with indignation. 'To see if I felt the same way as my mother?'

He didn't deny it, though his expression remained closed, inscrutable. 'I'm glad you feel the way you do,' he said impassively. Kelly had a feeling he really meant 'surprised' rather than 'glad'. Why should he be *glad*? 'Your mother found it claustrophobic, Mungo said. The silence and the isolation bothered her. I could have understood if it had bothered you in the same way. It's a far cry up here from the applause and the adulation of the crowd.'

She caught her breath, her frown deepening. 'You think I'm missing *that*?' How little he knew her! 'It was never the *adulation of the crowd*, as you call it, that attracted me to show-jumping.'

'Oh? What was it then? The pure love of horses?' The scepticism in his voice was tangible, as clear as the scorn in his eyes.

She regarded him in silence for a long moment, her eyes deeply violet in the shadow of the tall gums.

'You wouldn't understand,' she said finally, turning sharply away.

He caught her arm. Not roughly, but with a gentleness that alarmed her as much as if he had brutally man-handled her.

'Try me,' he invited.

Growingly aware of an increase in her pulse-rate, she composed herself before turning back. As she faced him again, she saw that the scorn in his eyes had gone—or was it merely cleverly masked?—leaving his expression as un-readable as before. No, not quite. There was an air about him—of waiting, of expectancy.

She drew in a deep breath. She wasn't sure she wanted to reveal her private thoughts to Blade Ryan. She would have to be careful not to say too much; careful not to leave herself open to his disdain.

'It's more than just a love of horses,' she began cautiously. Though her eyes were fixed to his face, she was looking, not at him now, but inward, her thoughts roving into the past. 'I was always horse-mad. You don't devote your life to horses unless you love them. But it's more than that. It's more to do with ——' she shrugged, searching for the word '—communication. I believe that communication is the—is the balancing-pole of life,' she confessed quietly. 'Without it, one end of life would outweigh the other.' She hesitated,

oddly embarrassed to find herself talking this way to Blade
Ryan, of all people; but when she saw him nod
imperceptibly, she finished the thought aloud. 'Without
communication, I believe that harmony—and therefore
happiness—is impossible.'

'You're talking of communication between you and your
horse, of course?' he probed gently. There was no
discernible mockery in his eyes, though because she could
never be sure of him, she feared it could leap back without
warning if she revealed herself too fully; particularly if she
went on to talk about communication between *people*—
individuals. Here, in this atmospheric forest, alone with
Blade Ryan, such talk could be dangerously potent.

'Of course,' she agreed with a shrug. Let it end there, she
pleaded silently, swallowing uneasily as her eyes collided
with his—and found, ridiculously, alarmingly, that she
couldn't pull them away. It was like being in the grip of a
powerful magnet.

Even in the growing darkness, the brilliance of his grey
eyes was undimmed, the thick black lashes a startling
contrast. The fine charcoal ring that circled the grey irises
was closer to black now in the shadow of the darkening
ghost gums. She felt a faint sense of unreality, a floating
sensation as his gaze held hers.

When he raised his hand and gently slid his fingers across
the slender column of her throat, she was powerless to stop
him, shivering involuntarily as his cool fingers touched her
bare skin. She could feel the fine hairs at the nape of her
neck rising under his touch, and her lips parted in an
unspoken protest. This was not what she wanted, and yet if
she didn't want it, why was she still standing there, why
didn't she turn away, why was she hardly daring to
breathe?

She was dimly conscious that he had moved a step
nearer, that he was now dangerously, suffocatingly close.
His thumb-tip was lightly caressing her throat, mesmeris-
ing her as surely as his grey hypnotic gaze. It was only with
a supreme effort that she managed to break the spell and
tug her eyes away, but as she tried to avert her face as well,

his hand slid round under her chin and tilted it upwards, his fingers forcing her head back to that she had nowhere else to look but into his eyes.

She knew he was going to kiss her, but she didn't struggle, reminding herself hazily that she had been kissed before and had always managed to remain in control, never allowing the situation to get out of hand, confident that her deepest emotions would remain untouched. Even Harvey Quinn's passionate kisses had failed to make her lose her head—or her heart. Her restraint had at times irritated and frustrated him, she knew, but he had respected her wishes, no doubt confident that he would succeed in breaking down her defences in time. His self-confidence had been noticeably dented when she had left him to come to Australia—probably for good, she had warned him. She had wanted to finish it there and then; she had known her feelings for Harvey simply weren't strong enough—never had been, never would be.

The touch of Blade Ryan's lips on hers drove all thought of Harvey Quinn from her mind. Though it was the lightest, briefest of kisses, the merest brushing of his lips on hers, she was conscious of a heart-stopping, almost awesome anticipation. He lifted his head briefly to look down at her, his eyes in the gathering darkness glowing like hot coals. She held her breath as he brought his head down again, his face blurring over hers as he kissed her again, testingly as before: once, twice, three times, light, teasing kisses that sent stabs of unexpected pleasure knifing through her.

Finally his lips took hers with a fierce demand that sent her senses spiralling. His mouth ground over hers, forcing her lips apart, his hand still holding her chin captive. As her body weakened in dazed reaction, she felt her own lips responding, softening under his. To save her legs buckling beneath her, she clutched instinctively at his jacket.

With his free arm he pushed aside her suede jacket and slid his arm round her waist, pulling her closer, his fingers digging into her flesh through the thin cotton of her shirt. As his lips left hers and moved downwards to explore the hollow of her throat, his hand fumbled with her shirt, his fingers slipping underneath to trail caressingly over her bare flesh. At his touch a new sensation pulsed through her, a throbbing sensation that rolled deep down into the pit of her stomach. She made a sound in her throat, a soft groan that brought an answering grunt—of pleasure? satisfaction?—from Blade. At the same time his hand stilled on her back. Raising his head, he looked down at her for a long moment. When he spoke, his tone was mocking.

'Won't you miss all this if you stay buried out here in the Australian bush? The attention of men, romance, your old glittering social life?'

With a stifled gasp, she wrenched herself free, pink spots of mingled shame and anger staining her cheeks. Oh God, she had fallen right into Blade Ryan's trap! She might have known he was only playing with her, that his own emotions wouldn't have been touched! He had kissed her merely as a kind of cruel test, to make her see what she would be missing by staying in Australia—in the isolation of Windarra Valley!

She forced her chin up, pride blazing in her eyes, dimming the hurt and the anger. 'On the contrary,' she said priding herself that she could keep her voice steady, when her emotions were still in a state of chaos, 'I'm not missing my old life one bit. With places like this,' she waved her hand at the ghostly gums towering above them, the clear air still filled with the musical call of the bell-birds, 'who could want more?' She added carelessly, somehow injecting a note of banter into her voice, 'The beauty and the grandeur is so spectacular, I think we both got a bit carried away by it,' stressing the word *both*. Let him think she was no more affected by what had happened than he was!

In the growing shadows, she couldn't read his expression. Nor did she wait around to try, rubbing her hands together as though suddenly discovering that she felt cold—cold and hungry.

'Where's that flask? I could do with some hot soup.'

They sat in the car to drink it, neither speaking much, the twittering of birds and the fluttering of wings filling any awkward silences. Not that anybody could feel truly awkward in such a place, Kelly reflected, breathing the crisp mountain air into her lungs through the open window. It as too magical for that.

Despite what had happened, despite the cruel trick he had played on her, it would for ever remain a magical place.

Blade stayed for a bite of dinner, but now that they were back at Windarra, they might have been polite strangers. Kelly kept the conversation firmly on neutral topics, and any stud matters they discussed were general ones, such as blood-lines and yearling sales and methods of training, not specific Windarra problems. She didn't want Blade Ryan thinking she couldn't cope without his help. More than ever now, she was determined to show him that she could run things as well as he—better! And she was equally determined never to fall into a trap of his making again.

He didn't stay long, for which Kelly was thankful, leaving immediately after they had eaten. Kelly saw him off at the door, not walking to the Land Rover with him.

She wondered if he was regretting that contrived kiss in the ghost-gum forest. Regretting the way it had misfired, no doubt! Assuming she had succeeded in convincing him that it had. Blade Ryan did not like to admit failure, she already knew that. And his failure to make her admit that she was missing her old life and the company of men must have annoyed him. He must be quietly kicking himself for bothering to take her to the forest in the first place! He had been hoping that she would find the place as alien and uninviting as her mother had—and his kiss had been intended only to heighten her feelings of homesickness. He had failed on both counts!

She preferred not to analyse her own emotions too deeply. Though his kiss hadn't succeeded in the way he had intended, it *had* affected her, there was no denying it. She still felt confused and dismayed at the way she had mindlessly responded, at the way she had allowed his kisses, his caresses, to arouse her. Maybe Blade Ryan's heartless little experiment had succeeded more truly than he knew—

maybe she *was* missing Harvey Quinn and the other men who had danced attendance on her during her travels around the world. Why else would she have reacted in such an emotional way? It certainly couldn't have been Blade Ryan himself who had inspired that treacherous response. She despised the man!

The next day she threw herself into her work with such gusto that she had no time or energy left over to think about Blade Ryan or what he might try next. She was gradually earning the trust and respect of the Windarra staff—even crusty old Joe McQueen. She could sense it as clearly as she could breathe in the fragrance of lilacs and roses that these days filled the house. It was a heart-warming feeling, only marred by the shadow of Blade Ryan waiting to swoop in triumphantly the moment she made a mistake or suffered a serious setback.

During the afternoon she took one of the stock-horses and rode out with Harry Watts to inspect the fences, enjoying the feeling of being back in the saddle again, but missing her beloved Pixie. She must try to find another mare to replace her—not for show-jumping, of course, but for her own use and enjoyment around the stud.

When she walked into the office late in the afternoon, she heard Mary Lou talking on the phone.

'Yes, all right, love, I'll try,' the girl was saying a trifle breathlessly. When she saw Kelly, she blushed furiously and with a quick 'have to go', she rang off.

Kelly smiled brightly, wondering if it had been Blade Ryan on the phone. *Love*, Mary Lou had called whoever had been on the line. She brutally ignored the pang that accompanied her smile. Why should it bother her if Blade Ryan and Mary Lou were romantically involved?

'I need to make a phone-call,' she said, sitting down at her own desk. 'I want to find out how Mrs Ryan is. She ought to be home by now.'

'You go ahead.' Mary Lou sprang from her chair as she spoke. No mention of Blade, or of Mrs Ryan either, Kelly noticed, eyeing the girl speculatively. Wouldn't she have

said something if she had just been speaking to Blade?
Unless they wanted to keep their friendship a secret! An
involvement between Windarra Stud's secretary and the
man who wanted to take Windarra Stud away from its new
owner . . .No, it was unlikely they'd want to spread that
around!

'Mind if I wander outside for a breather?' Mary Lou was
already heading for the door.

Kelly shook her head. 'Why don't you go down to the
stables and join the others? They were just stopping for
coffee when I left. You hardly see anyone, stuck in here in
the office all day.'

'Oh, I'll just take a walk . . . I prefer to leave the stables to
the menfolk.' With a wave of her manicured hand, Mary
Lou vanished through the open doorway.

Kelly smiled after her. The girl did work hard and she
deserved a break. Despite her preoccupation with her looks
and hair and the fact that she preferred not to mingle with
the stable staff—Blade would approve of that, she reflected
sourly: the fact that the girl didn't encroach on what he
would consider to be *men's* territory—despite all those little
feminine foibles Mary Lou had already proved to Kelly
that she was a reliable and efficient secretary, a valuable
asset to have around.

She found herself wondering idly if Blade Ryan had ever
kissed Mary Lou the way he had kissed her the previous
evening.

She squeezed her eyes shut, disgusted with herself. What
did she care who Blade Ryan kissed—or *how*? Anyway, she
was being pathetically naïve. If the two really were
romantically involved, their kisses were bound to have
gone much further than——

She cut off the thought with a shocked gasp, a rush of
colour sweeping her cheeks. What in the world was
happening to her, sinking to speculation of that nature?
Blade Ryan's personal life was of no earthly concern of
hers, of no possible interest to her!

She picked up the phone and dialled. When Blade

Ryan's voice answered, she had to swallow hard before she could speak.

'You're back,' she said, and realised how inane the words sounded. 'How is your mother?' she asked hastily. 'Did she have a comfortable flight home?'

'Yes. Mother's resting at present, she's rather tired and still a bit sore,' Blade said amiably. 'But she's coming along all right. We'll arrange another night to have you over to dinner. How about after the weekend?'

'Oh no, I wouldn't dream——' Kelly protested.

'She's keen to meet you,' Blade cut in. He had said that before, she recalled, frowning slightly, still not sure if Grace Ryan genuinely wanted to meet her, or simply felt it her duty to be courteous to a neighbour.

'I'd like to pop in some time to see how she's going on, and to meet her,' she heard herself answering. 'But let's forget about coming to dinner. I wouldn't even consider it, in the circumstances. But as soon as your mother feels up to it, I'd like to have you all over *here* for dinner.'

Now what in the world had made her say that? *All* of them? That meant Grace Ryan and Blade Ryan and Blade's sister Megan and Megan's fiancé Dan Cassidy: the whole Bilba tribe! What had possessed her to issue an invitation like that? It would be like inviting a bunch of ravening vultures to dinner!

She flushed guiltily at the thought, and was glad Blade couldn't see her face. She was being unfair. Windarra and Bilba were close neighbours, and they would have to learn to live in harmony together, however much the Ryans might want to get their hands on Windarra. Inviting them all for dinner would show them she was serious about staying, and that they might as well forget their ambition to own Windarra. Because she *was* going to stay, she was becoming surer of that by the minute. Just as she was sure her father would have *wanted* her to stay and run the place herself; that he would have wanted to keep Windarra in his family. Whether she was going to be able to run the place as successfully as he... She shook off her doubts. Why not? She felt a tremble of excitement. She had never shrunk from a challenge in the past. Why now? If Blade Ryan tried

any more clever little ploys to make her change her mind—
if he put any deliberate obstacles in her path—he would
have a fight and a half on his hands. He didn't know what
he was up against!

'Very kind of you,' Blade drawled, and she was thankful
she couldn't see *his* face! She had the uneasy feeling he could
be planning to use the occasion for purposes of his own. To
show her up in front of his family, perhaps? Here on her
home ground, where her shortcomings would be more
glaringly obvious? Hoping to deflate her, if she knew Blade
Ryan, so that she would want to give up and go home!

Let him try!

'In the meantime,' she realised Blade was saying, in a
prompt change of subject, as though he had been thinking
nothing of the sort, 'have you decided if you're flying down
to the Caulfield Cup with me tomorrow?'

The Caulfield Cup! Of course, tomorrow was Saturday.
It had come so quickly!

'Well, I'd like to go,' she said slowly. 'Um, is anyone else
flying down with you?'

'No,' he said, sounding mildly amused. 'Megan's staying
here to look after Mother.'

'Then let's fly down in my father's Piper Cherokee. You
can give me some instructions on the way. I'd like to learn
how to fly.' It was high time she started calling some of the
tunes, telling Blade Ryan what *she* wanted instead of the
other way round!

There was a brief, palpable silence before his impassive
reply. 'If you like.'

'Thank you. What time will you be here?'

'I'll pick you up at nine-thirty. We'll fly down to Sydney
and catch a commercial flight from there on to Melbourne.
I'll arrange the air tickets. We'll be flying back to Sydney
later in the day, but it may be too late to fly from there back
to Windarra. We have no landing-lights, remember, at
either Windarra or Bilba. So bring an overnight bag just in
case.'

He hung up before she could comment, before she could even react. An overnight stay in Sydney with Blade Ryan? *Hell!*

She sighed heavily. Why did she have the feeling she was losing control again—being manipulated, come to that? It was not a feeling she was used to—and for sure, not one she relished!

She woke early. It was cool, crisp, sunny morning without a breath of wind. A perfect day for flying. But there was work to do first in the stables. She would be away for the remainder of the day, and possibly part of tomorrow as well, and she had no wish to add to Joe McQueen's already heavy workload.

Later, with a couple of busy hours behind her, she returned to the house to shower and change.

She was waiting on the front steps, her overnight bag packed and ready beside her, when Blade arrived just before nine thirty. He threw open the door of the Land Rover even before the vehicle had come to a complete halt.

'Throw it in the back,' he commanded, revving the engine. No *good morning, how are you?*, she noted sourly. As she scrambled in beside him, she tossed her bag behind her.

'Good morning,' she said impassively, to show him she was not intimidated. Let him throw his weight around as much as he pleased! If his idea was to make her want to run home to Mother, he hadn't a hope in the world! She had never been a weakling—and she was certainly no wilting cry-baby!

Blade wasted no time bundling her aboard the neat little Cherokee, and in minutes they were off the ground, soaring over the patchwork paddocks of Windarra Stud.

'Would you explain how you did that?' Kelly asked when he gave no sign that he had remembered her request of the night before. 'I want to learn how to fly this thing.'

He turned his head lazily, and with a shrug, rapped out a few instructions, his tone sardonic.

She compressed her lips. He doesn't want to teach me, she thought, because he doesn't want me to stay.

Catching her look, he gave a sigh and said, 'If you're

really determined to learn how to fly, you might as well do it properly. Apply for a student pilot's permit and be prepared to have regular lessons——'

'I intend to do just that,' she said with a toss of her head. 'Do you think Joe would give me some lessons? Is he qualified to teach?'

'Joe's far too busy—I wouldn't even ask him. If you're really serious, I'll teach you myself.' There was nothing gracious about his offer. She wondered why he even bothered. 'There's more to it than just learning how to use the controls. You have to learn about aerodynamics, maintenance, meteorology, navigation, safety checks, flying regulations, the lot. You can learn most of that on the ground. Watch me now, by all means. I'll explain a few things as we go along. But if you want to learn properly we'll have to arrange a regular time together—say, Sunday mornings. If you can spare the time.' Something she didn't altogether trust kindled in his eyes.

'You'd be prepared to give me lessons every Sunday morning?' she asked warily. What would he want in return?

'If you can spare the time,' he repeated pleasantly.

She eyed him suspiciously. If *she* could spare the time. Was he secretly hoping that she would spend so much time indulging her whim to fly that she would neglect Windarra? And then, when she found it was all too much to handle and decided to sell up and leave, would Blade Ryan be waiting to dive in to the rescue—with an offer to buy her out?

She sighed. 'I'll make the time,' she said stiffly. 'Thanks.' She mustn't dwell on his possible motives, she must think only of what it was going to mean to be able to fly her father's plane. It would mean independence ... convenience. Relaxation too, perhaps. She had seen Blade Ryan's exultation at the controls, and she wanted to feel that same elation, that same freedom.

'Right.' Blade tapped the control-stick. 'A few rudimentary points. Just sit back and listen. Listen and observe.'

She sat back, listening and observing, until they arrived

at Sydney Airport, where, after checking her overnight bag into a locker for convenience, they boarded an airbus bound for Melbourne. Inside the aircraft a Titian-haired stewardess greeted Blade with a dazzling smile and a cry of delight.

'Blade Ryan! I haven't seen you since you mortified us all by giving up flying. How *are* you? Bored to tears yet with that horse-stud of your?' As Blade, with the barest of smiles, shook his head, she swayed towards him, lowering her voice. 'I'm having the night off when we reach Melbourne. How about getting together, for old time's sake? Remember the good times we used to have?'

'Sorry, we're coming back to Sydney immediately after the Caulfield Cup,' Blade told her, his tone cool.

'*We?*' Looking beyond him, the girl saw Kelly standing behind. 'Well.' Her red lips curved into a knowing smile. 'It has to be Rowena Shaw's daughter. I've seen all her films, and I saw your photograph in the papers last week,' she told Kelly. 'Quite an inheritance, if you're into horse-farms. Well, you two didn't take long to get together, did you? Blade always did have an eye for a pretty girl.' Her dark eyes glowed. With malevolence? Envy? Spite?

'We're neighbours,' Kelly said swiftly, frowning slightly. She had no wish to remain standing around gossiping with one of Blade Ryan's old flames.

Blade apparently had the same thought. 'We'd better find our seats,' he said with a curtness that suggested he didn't think much of his old flame. As he swung round to lead the way, the stewardess caught Kelly's arm.

'You'll never tame Blade Ryan,' she warned in a knowing undertone. 'He'll love you and leave you. When Blade settles down—*if* he ever does—it won't be with a good-looking girl like you. I think he secretly despises glamorous, independent women.' A peevish look burned in the girl's dark eyes. 'If he chooses anyone, it'll be a passive, fluffy little thing who'll be content to stay at home on the farm like his mother always did and who won't die of boredom living in the bush, who'll be content with her babies and her farmhouse and her husband's occasional presence.'

'I wouldn't know,' Kelly said and hurried on, closing her ears to any more—though the girl had summed up Blade Ryan pretty well, she thought with a wry twist of her lips. Hadn't she suspected much the same herself? Why it should cause a faint twinge to hear someone else voicing those same thoughts she couldn't imagine. *She* certainly had no designs on the man! He was a grasping, ruthless, infuriating, domineering male chauvinist who liked throwing his weight around and making all the decisions, regardless of what anyone else—let alone a mere woman!—might want herself. She would never want a man like that. He was worse than Harvey Quinn! Harvey might have put himself and his winning first, but at least he had always respected her—and he had loved her too, in his own way.

Neither mentioned the stewardess as they settled into their seats. For a while they chatted about racing, and later, over a cup of tea, Blade told her something that surprised her. She was surprised by both *what* he told her, and by the fact that he, Blade Ryan, thought actually to mention it at all.

'I think you've won Joe over,' he drawled, his dark-lashed eyes half closed, masking his own thoughts. 'He thinks you're a chip off the old block.'

'You mean——'

'I mean he thinks you take after your father—that you're a lot like him. From Joe that's quite a compliment.'

It was indeed. She couldn't resist asking, 'And what do *you* think?'

'I think you've shown that you're perfectly capable of running the place,' he said, surprising her further. She had a feeling, however, that a 'but' was coming, and jumped in first.

'As well as any woman can, you mean.'

'As well as any man,' he said, and laughed at her astonished look.

'But there's something still bugging you,' she accused, a

frown puckering her brow.

He nodded. 'Capable or not, you still haven't convinced me you'll stick it out.'

She heaved a sigh. She might have known! 'You think I'll be like my mother,' she said bitterly. 'And yet you just said yourself that I'm more like my father.'

'No. Joe said that. Now don't get mad,' he begged, throwing up a defensive hand. 'I'm not thinking of your mother. I'm thinking of *you*. You're young, you're new to all this, you're new to this *country*, and you've spent a long time in a totally different world, in the limelight, travelling constantly, always surrounded by other people. How can you be sure you *won't* miss all that in time—that you won't get fed up with the isolation and the hard work and the loneliness out here?'

She threw back her head, meeting him eye to eye. 'Because those things you mentioned—being forever in the public eye, the travelling from place to place—never meant as much to me as Windarra has come to mean in just this short time.'

He looked at her speculatively. 'You really speak as if you mean that.' But there was still doubt in his voice.

'I do mean it.' Her eyes narrowed. 'I hope it won't upset *your* plans too much. There must be other properties, other valleys. I'm sure you'll get lucky and find a place that will satisfy you as much as Windarra Stud.'

He didn't answer that. But his brow shot up in an expressive gesture. He was still hoping it wouldn't be necessary to look for another place, damn him! *How can you be sure you won't get fed up in time?* he'd said. *Ooh!* It made her hands itch to reach out and wring his arrogant neck!

'Let me tell you about Melbourne,' Blade said with an infuriating smile, as if he knew his neck was perfectly safe.

On the return flight to Sydney later in the day—much later than they had originally intended—neither spoke much; they both had too much on their minds. Kelly was remembering the unbelievable thrill of Heathcote's stunning win, while at the same time her heart went out to

Blade, and to his gallant horse Sherwin, who had pulled up lame at the finish, having battled gamely on to finish second after being kicked early in the race.

Blade had been philosophical about it, hiding his disappointment.

'Sherwin likes to race from behind, but it gets him into trouble at times when he can't get a clear run. The kick he had today was an accident—just one of the hazards of racing.'

Kelly's mind drifted back to the early part of the day, to the excitement of meeting her father's fiery bay champion Heathcote for the first time. And later, in the saddling-paddock before the running of the Caulfield Cup, she had met Heathcote's jockey, Wayne Black, wearing the Heath colours, blue, red and gold. It was here that she had her first glimpse too of Blade Ryan's magnificent chestnut horse, Sherwin, and met Sherwin's red-headed strapper Mike, and Blade's younger brother Ambler, who was Sherwin's trainer.

Ambler had stared at her with unabashed surprise as they shook hands.

'You look so much like your mother—or the way she looked twenty-odd years ago. I don't remember her all that well, but Angie and I saw one of her early films on television last week. Your mother hated the valley,' he stated baldly. 'She hated the whole set-up out here. Do you think you'll be able to stick it out?'

The direct approach. These Ryan men pulled no punches!

'If my father managed to stick it out,' she replied sweetly, shifting the emphasis away from her mother, 'I'm sure I will too. I may look like my mother, but I'd say I am more like my father—as Joe McQueen already concedes and Blade is beginning to find out,' she added, challenging Blade with her eyes.

Blade had acknowledged the look with an enigmatic smile and a decided glint in his eye, as if to say 'Convince me.'

Both, however, had congratulated her with what

appeared to be genuine pleasure when Heathcote—*her* horse—won the Caulfield Cup, the valuable first leg of the Caulfield-Melbourne Cup double. Heathcote's trainer Max Beatty had then dragged Kelly to the presentation ceremony to recieve the Cup personally from the Governor of Victoria. She even had to make a short speech, which was received with loud applause, as if the Australian people were prepared to accept her into their ranks. It was a heart-warming moment, marred only by the thought of the unfortunate injury suffered by the Ryan's horse Sherwin, which must have affected her chance of winning. She had no wish to win in such a way!

Sherwin's leg was found to be badly bruised and swollen. Ambler and Blade, after conferring together, decided it would be wise to send him back to Bilba for a spell.

'He should be full recovered in time to run in the Melbourne Cup in November,' Blade said, relieving the worry that had been on all their minds. 'He's had some hard races lately. A spell won't do him any harm.'

They had intended leaving Melbourne immediately after the Caulfield Cup, but Heathcote's win and Sherwin's injury delayed their departure. By the time they arrived in Sydney it was far too late to fly back to Windarra in the Cherokee that same evening.

As Kelly had feared, it meant spending the night at the Ryans' apartment in the city, a prospect that filled her with dread, though she accepted the inevitability of it, on the surface at least, with composure. It was the kind of thing that must happen frequently to the Ryans. When one relied on light planes and airstrips without night-lights, one had to be prepared for overnight stopovers occasionally. Fogs and storms were another hazard that could have grounded them for the night. It was nothing to get excited about. Just one of those things.

CHAPTER SIX

THEY had coffee at the airport terminal before picking up Kelly's overnight bag and catching a taxi into the city. Neither wanted dinner, having had a generous meal on the plane. On their way into town Blade offered to take her to King's Cross to visit some of Sydney's well known nightspots, if she felt like celebrating her win that way; but she declined with a shake of her head. It had been a long day, and she felt she could do without nightclubs, and she sensed that Blade, with his worry over Sherwin, wasn't in the mood either.

As a compromise, Blade directed their driver to cruise slowly through the neon-lit streets of King's Cross to give Kelly a passing glimpse of the weird, colourful sights that made 'Australia's Montmarte', as Blade described King's Cross, such a famous attraction. Or should it be *in*famous? Kelly wondered as they drove along. Punks with spiky heads prowled in packs. Painted women in tight skirts lolled suggestively in doorways. Shuffling tourists, noosed with cameras, swarmed past the bright, gaudy windows, while bellowing spruikers tried to entice into their dubious dens whoever was passing by. Kelly had an impression of a garish, gross, electric world—a world without subtelety or pretence.

Afterwards, again at Blade's command, they drove across the massive Sydney Harbour Bridge to Milson's Point to view the city lights from across the water and to watch the twinkling ferries chugging by. The shimmering reflections on the water and the illuminated Opera House—an incredible structure, looking like a spectacular white swan settling into the water—plucked a cry of delight from Kelly's lips.

'It's beautiful! Breath-taking!'

Blade looked down at her, his eyes in the soft darkness

glowing with an expression she wasn't game to examine too closely. *I can be persuasive*, he had said once. She mustn't fall into another of his silken traps!

'A little more exhilarating than the nightclubs of King's Cross—I agree,' he murmured. 'Breathe in the air . . . no smoke, no sweaty bodies, no loud music. You made a wise choice.'

Rare praise, from Blade Ryan! She smiled up at him, surprised at how pleased she felt. *Careful, Kelly Heath. Remember what this man wants from you.*

By the time they reached the Ryan's apartment building both were yawning and ready for bed, Kelly retreating with nervous haste into the room allotted to her.

But she found she couldn't sleep. Whether it was the excitement of Heathcote's win, or her concern over Sherwin's condition, or the disturbing proximity of Blade Ryan, with only a thin partition separating them, she couldn't have said. Most likely a combination of all three.

As the hours dragged by, with sleep still evading her, she gave up trying, deciding that a stroll round the apartment might help. She opened her door and listened. Hearing no sound, she crept out.

A narrow shaft of light fell across the carpet from a gap between the heavy drapes. The rest of the room was in darkness.

She followed the shaft of light to the long windows and stood looking out at the blinking windows opposite.

A sound in the room caused her to stiffen. A board creaked behind her, and she felt cool fingers close over her bare shoulders.

She didn't breathe, didn't move. She didn't seem able to.

'You couldn't sleep either?' Blade's voice was tormentingly close; she could feel his warm breath on the back of her neck, his lips in her hair.

She breathed in deeply before answering, not sure she could trust her voice.

'I'm afraid not,' she managed finally, still not moving, not attempting to turn and face him. 'You'd think I'd be used to strange beds by now,' she said with an unsteady laugh. So Blade couldn't sleep either. Was he still worried about Sherwin? She found herself wanting to stay and comfort him.

Was that why she didn't pull away, why she didn't run for her life? she wondered bemusedly. Or was it only a lame excuse, a weak justification for the strange inertia that was sweeping over her, parlaysing her limbs?

'Oh? Have you been in many strange beds? Whose, I wonder?' he mocked softly, deliberately misunderstanding. Unless ..., she felt herself stiffening. Unless he hadn't misunderstood at all. Unless he was thinking of her mother again. The unfaithful wife who, Blade seemed to believe, had raised her daughter to be as immoral as herself!

My mother was never promiscuous, she felt like blurting out. She fell in love with Chuck Nagle while she was still married to Mungo Heath, that's true—but she has been happily married to Chuck for well over twenty years and has never looked at another man in all that time!

Instead she said, irritation sharpening her voice, 'I've spent years travelling the world and if I have spent any of that time in anyone else's bed I don't see that it is any of your business! How would you like it if I asked you the same question!'

He laughed softly, causing a prickling sensation along her spine. 'It would be too much to expect, I guess, that——' he cut the rest off abruptly, his grip tightening on her shoulders, swinging her round to face him.

Alarm tugged at her throat. 'Let me go!' She tried to pull free then, but he crushed her to him, making her trembingly aware that, other than the briefest of shorts, he was naked. She could feel her heart pounding in rhythm with his as his hard-muscled chest strained against her soft curves and the heat of his body burned through the flimsy silk of her nightgown.

His head came down and his mouth captured hers, his lips sensual and demanding, choking her of breath. At the same time she was conscious of his hand on her lower back, pressing her to him, arousing piquant needles of pleasure deep inside her.

Alarmed as she was at the emotions spiralling through her, she had lost all thought of struggling free. Her limbs had turned to honey, warm and sweet and melting, robbbing her of her strength. Through her thin nightgown his chest, thrust up against hers, felt warm and moist. Fire throbbed through her breasts, and she could feel her nipples hardening against his burning skin. A ragged sigh was wrung from her lips.

The hand low on her back crushed her even closer, and now she could feel something else that alarmed her even more.

'No,' she moaned, but she couldn't find the energy to pull away.

Breathing heavily, Blade drew back his head and looked down at her, the fingers of his other hand slipping the strap of her gown from her shoulder, peeling it away to reveal a rounded pearly breast. A flame licked down her body as his fingers touched it gently.

'God, you're beautiful!' he murmured, and buried his lips in the soft hollow of her throat. Slowly his mouth moved downwards, over the soft mound of her breast, feathering hot kisses over her fiery flesh, his tongue flicking out to inflame her senses with each delicate touch. As his lips reached her taut nipple her body arched instinctively against him, the flicking of his tongue sending a rush of intense heat through her.

At the same time he let his fingers trail lightly down her body, way, way down to areas she had never allowed any man to touch before. Deep shudders pulsed through her, and she felt a singing in her ears, like the rising rush of a sea breeze.

No man, she thought wildly, mindlessly pressing her fiery body against his. No man has ever . . .

But this wasn't just any man, she realised foggily . . . this was Blade Ryan, her adversary, her *enemy*, the man who wanted to buy her out! He was trying to break down her defences so that she would willingly do anything he asked, give him anything he wanted. He didn't want *her*, he only wanted what she could give him!

My God, what was she doing?

'No!' This time it was a definite no—a strangled little cry though it was. She struggled in his arms, her strength seeping back, agonisingly slowly, into her paralysed limbs.

His head came up, his eyes seeking hers in the dimness, eyes still dazed with desire. She saw a note of enquiry as well—and something else that might have been anger. For a moment his arms tightened around her, as though he would fight to subdue her, but as she continued to struggle, more violently now, as she wrenched her arms free and began to lash out at him, he pushed her away, standing boldly in front of her in the shaft of light, not attempting to hide his arousal—or his anger.

'So this is the way you treat your men, is it?' he accused, his voice like the lash of a whip. 'Teasing them, leading them on, then pulling away at the last moment! Or is it only *me* you pull away from—because you're not sure if I want *you*—or what *belongs* to you? Well, let me tell you something, Kelly Nagle Heath—I know that I want Windarra! I wonder if you want it as much?' He swung on his heel and disappeared, panther-like, into the darkness. Seconds later she heard his door slam shut.

The air remained filled with his anger, cutting deep into her heart—though why it should she couldn't imagine. He was despicable! Hadn't he just admitted that he didn't want *her*—that it was Windarra Stud he wanted? No doubt he thought that by having her first he could more easily get his hands on Windarra! She was lucky she had fought him off before it was too late. He could have forced himself on her, of course, as it had seemed for a moment that he might; but he had thought twice about that. He would have lost Windarra—lost any dim chance he might have had—if he had taken her against her will; he had realised that just in time.

What he didn't know—what he steadfastly refused to accept—was that he had already lost any chance of getting his hands on Windarra. She had already committed herself. And now that she had made up her own mind to stay, there would be no changing it. If she had had any lingering

doubts before, today had laid them to rest. Not so much
what had happened just now, with Blade, but what had
taken place earlier in the day. Heathcote's great win in the
Caulfield Cup had given her the boost she needed,
confirming in her own mind that she had made the right
decision. With that one win, she had gained confidence,
money, prestige, and with Heathcote's stud prospects, a
rosy future as well. And Blade Ryan wasn't going to take
any of that away from her!

She tiptoed back to her room and slipped between the
rumpled sheets; but still she couldn't sleep, the memory of
Blade's fiery caresses, his half-naked body pressed against
her, his steamy skin burning through the thin fabric of her
nightgown—and its electrifying effect on her—still vivid
in her mind. When she did finally drop off, the first rays of
dawn were already streaking the sky.

A knock on her door woke her. She was instantly,
apprehensively, awake, grabbing the sheet before she
answered.

'I'm awake. I'll be out in a minute. Don't come in!'

'I won't come in,' Blade's voice drawled, his tone
unmistakably dry. 'Ready for breakfast?'

'Yes—no! I'll have a quick shower and get dressed first.'

'Fine.' He couldn't resist his usual autocratic last word.
'I've booked a cab for nine o'clock. It's after eight now.'

'I'll be ready.' She resisted the impulse to snap. Play it
cool. Show him that nothing he does or says can affect you.
Pretend last night never happened.

Within fifteen minutes she had showered and changed
into the jeans and shirt she had brought with her for the
flight home. She had left her face untouched, only brushing
her hair.

When she came out she could smell toast. It smelt good.
On the table was a glass of freshly squeezed orange juice
and an empty plate with a dish of butter and honey beside
it.

'It's not much,' Blade muttered, rescuing the toast from
the automatic toaster. 'There's not much in the fridge at the

moment, and there was only frozen bread.'

'Looks good to me,' she said, matching his neutral tone, avoiding his eyes as she reached for her glass of orange juice. How polite they were this morning!

She felt his eyes on her as she buttered her toast.

'I want to apologise for last night,' he said abruptly.

Blade Ryan, *apologising*! She took a deep breath, and released it slowly.

'There's no need,' she said finally, in a small voice. It had been as much her fault, just as it had been in the ghost-gum forest the other evening. What was wrong with her, that she went to water whenever he touched her!

Blade spoke again. 'I'm afraid I may have misjudged you.' There was no expression in his voice, or in his face. At least there was no discernible mockery or derision either.

She gave him a questioning look. He couldn't be finding this easy. Admitting he had misjudged a woman! She waited, saying nothing.

'I thought you came out of your room last night because you knew I was out here . . . that you'd heard me come out earlier.'

Her lips parted, her eyes showing her astonishment, and swift denial.

He added steadily, 'When I touched you and you made no move to break away, I assumed——'

She hushed him with a quick, 'Please, Blade,' trying to fight down her rising colour. 'I didn't know you were out here, but—you're right. It was my fault. I should never——' she broke off. Now it was she who was apologising—she who had never apologised to any man, not even Harvey Quinn, the man she had walked out on.

'Let's not say any more. 'A ghost of a smile played about Blade's lips. 'We were both a bit emotional last night—you with Heathcote winning, me with Sherwin getting hurt.'

Kelly nodded. Of course, that was all it was. They had both been over-tired and emotional. 'I was as concerned as you were about Sherwin,' she admitted soberly. 'I didn't want Heathcote to win at Sherwin's expense. I wanted him to win fair and square.'

'He did win fair and square. That's racing. You have to be prepared for things like that. They happen all the time.'

They were back on safer ground, and that was where they remained for the rest of the morning, until they were safely back at Windarra, Blade having given her a few more tips on flying the Cherokee on the way. After he had dropped her off at the house and driven of, she threw herself into Windarra matters, determined to keep her mind off what had happened last night.

The following afternoon, as she was heading back to the house from the stables, she heard the clip-clop of hooves and saw a horse and rider emerge from the row of poplars. It was Blade, on a spirited black gelding.

She felt herself stiffening with nervous apprehension.

'Good afternoon.' He had seen her.

'Hi.' She ran her tongue nervously along her lips to moisten their sudden dryness. She was remembering the intimate touch of his hands on her lightly-clad body, his plundering mouth on her.

No! She mustn't think about it! He had apologised for what had happened. He wanted to forget it—so must she.

She made a fuss of the gelding as he pulled up alongside, so that she didn't have to look up at him.

'He's a beauty. What's his name?'

'Sinbad. He was a great racehorse in his day. He was retired about five years ago and I bought him for my own use.'

'How's Sherwin?' she asked, risking a glance upwards. The sun made her squint and she raised her hand, glad of an excuse to shield her eyes from his gaze. He was looking amused, damn him!

This is crazy, she thought in exasperation. When have I ever been afraid to look a man directly in the eye?

'He's badly bruised, but the swelling's going down, thank God.' Blade's eyes swerved away as he swung down from the saddle. 'He's quite enjoying being pampered and having a break from his daily workout. It won't do him any harm.' Now he was standing directly in front of her, his shadow falling across her face so that she had no excuse now to shield her eyes or to squint. But she felt composed enough by now to face him eye to eye.

'That's good news. Are you staying?' she asked. Realising how abrupt that sounded, she added hastily, 'If you are, I'll get Harry or Nico to look after Sinbad for you.'

'No need. I actually came to ask you over to Bilba.' Kelly's heart gave a tiny lurch. 'You mentioned you wanted to pop in and see Mother, so I thought I'd ride over and see if you'd like to ride back with me. I can see that you don't lose your way.'

'That's good of you. How *is* your mother?' Kelly wished she could be surer of Blade Ryan's motives. Was this just another of his attempts to get her 'on side', so that if she did decide to sell Windarra, she would sell to him—to the Ryans?

'She's feeling much better.'

'That's good. Give me a minute to tell Elsie and Mary Lou, then I'll saddle a horse and be with you.'

He caught her arm. 'How about I go and see Elsie and Mary Lou for you? I want to have a word with Mary Lou anyway. You go and find yourself a horse. Here, mind taking Sinbad with you? He could do with a drink.'

She looked up at him quizzically. Why would Blade Ryan want a word with *her* private secretary? There was no longer any need for him to involve himself in Windarra Stud affairs, now that she, Kelly, was here. Or was he involved *personally* with Mary Lou? Was that what she was waiting to hear?

As if I care, she thought. And then, contrarily, damn it, I *do* care! Not because I'm interested in Blade Ryan myself, heaven forbid! I just don't want that man pushing his nose into Windarra any more than he has already—wheedling his way into my private secretary's affections—or her confidence, or whatever he's attempting to do. Undermining my authority here.

She realised she was still standing there, waiting for some kind of explanation. I have a right to know, she told herself defensively. Mary Lou is a Windarra employee. More than that—she's my confidential secretary!

'You want to see my secretary?' she asked at last, her tone cool.

He nodded, shrugging. 'Just a private matter,' he said. Their eyes met as he handed her the reins. She could have kicked herself when she saw the taunting look in his eyes. Surely he didn't think she was *jealous*? She had better disabuse him of that idea right here and now!

'Oh, is that all,' she said, feigning a lack of interest. 'I thought you might have had some outstanding business with my secretary that I should know about.'

His eyes were now laughing openly at her. Didn't he believe her? Or did he find it amusing that she should want to know what his 'outstanding business' was with her secretary? Did he think it was none of her concern?

As he strode off towards the house, she led Sinbad away, calling out to the swarthy Nico when she saw him, 'Saddle me a horse, will you, Nico? I'm going to Bilba to see Mrs Ryan. Um——' she chewed on her lip. 'And water Sinbad, will you, while I fetch my jacket from the house.' Although it was a fine afternoon, there was a growing chill in the air. Or was she just looking for an excuse to go back to the house?

She sighed. Why was she forever in two minds lately, for ever ready to make excuses to herself? She had always been so clear-minded in the past.

As she slipped in by the side door, she heard Blade's resonant voice talking to Elsie Duncan in the kitchen. Had he already been to see Mary Lou? She darted up the stairs to her room. Running a comb through her hair and touching up her lipstick—for Grace Ryan's benefit, not Blade's, she assured her reflection in the mirror—she threw her suede jacket over her shirt and jeans and hastened down the stairs to the kitchen. Elsie was there alone. Spying Kelly, she pushed a brown-paper package into her hands.

'For Mrs Ryan. I've been baking. I was about to give it to Blade.'

'Thanks, Elsie. I'll take a few of our baby tomatoes too.' When she left the kitchen she heard Blade's voice wafting from the direction of the office—calling goodbye to Mary Lou.

'See you tonight—I'm looking forward to it,' he said, and she heard his footsteps clattering over the polished boards towards her. Tonight? Kelly flicked her tongue over her lips. So they *were* involved—they *were* seeing each other!

When Blade caught sight of her his brow shot up. 'I've already told Elsie and Mary Lou I'm taking you to Bilba. Ready?'

Was he hoping that she hadn't overheard his parting words to Mary Lou? It was unlikely that he would want to broadcast the fact that he was involved in a relationship with Windarra Stud's private secretary—he wouldn't want to risk antagonising *her*, Kelly. Not while he still had that burning ambition to own Windarra Stud.

'I came back for my jacket,' she said hastily. 'And Elsie gave me these.' She held out her packages. He didn't think she'd come back to *spy* on him, she hoped! *Had* she? She hardly knew herself!

She strode ahead of him to the stables, kicking herself mentally for coming back to the house at all. Better to freeze all afternoon than have Blade Ryan think she had come back to check up on him! Or worse, to have him think she had been checking up, not out of idle curiosity, but out of jealousy! Which was probably precisely what he wanted her to feel! If he imagined she had a soft spot in her heart for him, how he must be gloating! All the easier, he must be thinking, to prise Windarra from her pliant fingers!

Ha! she scoffed under her breath. If he thought that, let him! She knew better!

Nico had their mounts ready. He had saddled a sorrel mare that Kelly had ridden once before. The mare wasn't Pixie, but she was a likeable, good-natured substitute.

Once she was in the saddle, once they were on their way, Kelly felt her nervous tension gradually slipping away. It was a pleasant ride to Bilba. The songs of the magpies accompanied their voices as they chatted over a range of safe topics—until Kelly, feeling in control of herself again, asked banteringly, 'I'm surprised you have so much time to spare on a mere neighbour. Aren't you busy at Bilba?'

He cocked an eyebrow at her. 'Perhaps I'm just super-efficient,' he said, his lip curving in a way that made her want to hit him. She *did* hit back—verbally.

'Or is it your stud-man Dan Cassidy who's the efficient one—so efficient that he can run the place without you,' she taunted, wanting to wipe the smirk from his face.

'Dan *is* efficient,' he agreed. 'I'll have no compunction about leaving him permanently in charge of Bilba.'

She had let herself wide open for that one. She fought down her anger to ask sweetly, 'Shouldn't you be looking around for another property?'

'Plenty of time.'

Those were the actual words he uttered, but he seemed to be saying something totally different with his eyes—those startling silver-grey eyes that glinted in the sunlight like the blade of a sword. He seemed to be saying, *I'll bide my time.* And a bit more besides. Like 'I know you'll sell Windarra Stud when the novelty wears off and the boredom sets in or when things get too tough for you, and then it won't be *necessary* for me to look around. Windarra will fall into my lap!'

Oh, no it won't, Blade Ryan!

'We're on Ryan property now,' Blade announced, and Kelly was thankful for the diversion. She was beginning to get emotional again!

The Bilba paddocks were extensive, the white-railed fences stretching as far as the eye could see, with mares and foals, colts and fillies, happily at home in the rich pastures. As they passed through the main gates—tall, impressive iron gates painted black with a gold trim—their conversation lulled, Kelly's interested gaze taking in the clipped lawns, the neat flower-beds alive with colour and scent, the sweeping circular driveway, and the neatly swept paths. Ahead, shadowed by a mantle of huge oaks and ashes, stood the white-walled homestead, a riot of wisteria clinging lovingly to the black shutters on the second storey above the columned verandas.

The sound of their horses' hooves had alerted Blade's

sister Megan, who was waiting to meet them when they rode into the courtyard at the rear of the house.

'Hi, Megan.' Blade greeted her in a softer tone than Kelly had ever heard him greet *her*. 'This is Kelly.'

'Hello, Kelly. Glad you could come over.' The girl's hair was hidden by a three-cornered red scarf and she was wearing brown drill overalls and a fawn shirt.

Smiling, Kelly sprang from her horse. As she landed in front of Blade's sister, the sun shone directly into her eyes, splintering the deep blue into fragments of glistening sapphire and violet and turquoise.

'Blade said you were beautiful—he was right,' Megan said matter-of-factly. She was a tall girl, big-boned and fresh-cheeked, with wisps of brown hair poking from the red scarf and warm brown eyes below. She looked nothing like her grey-eyed, tawny-haired brother; she was more like her younger brother Ambler. Kelly thought her rather plain until she smiled . . . a smile that transformed the girl's entire face, making it glow with an incandescent beauty. Kelly swallowed—hard. She was thinking of another smile, and what that other smile did to someone else's face, on the rare occasions she had been permitted to see it.

'Come and meet Mother,' Megan said, tucking her arm through Kelly's. 'She's on the patio.'

'I'll be in the stables,' said Blade, leading the two horses away. 'Bring Kelly down later, if you like, to see Sherwin.'

'The patio's just around here, by the pool.' Megan steered Kelly along a shaded path, fragrant with heady scents. They found Grace Ryan reclining, legs outstretched, on a banana lounger, a yellow umbrella shading her from the sun. A turquoise pool a few metres away looked refreshingly inviting, even on this crisp spring afternoon.

'Please don't get up,' Kelly said as Grace Ryan, with one hand encased in plaster, swung her legs round at their approach. Kelly saw at once where Megan's round, fresh-faced looks came from, and her serene smile. Grace's soft hair was grey now, but must have been brown like Megan's once.

'No, Mother, don't get up. We'll sit down here, next to

you.' Megan pulled up two canvas chairs. 'Mother won't admit it, but she's still a bit stiff after her fall.' She didn't mention her mother's arthritis, which Kelly suspected would have made rising doubly difficult. Blade, she recalled, had said his mother disliked talking about her disability.

Kelly burrowed into the bag on her shoulder. 'Elsie baked you some cookies,' she said, 'and I've also brought you some of our home-grown baby tomatoes.' She held out the two bulging paper bags and Grace took them from her, setting them down beside her.

'How kind of you both. Do thank Elsie—and thank you too, dear.' Grace held out her good hand to Kelly. 'You take me back—way back, to the days when your mother was here. You look so like her. I'm sorry your father died before you could meet him. Mungo loved to read about your successes, and he was deeply moved by the photographs of you in a recent magazine. He was overcome that you looked so much like your mother and yet had *his* love of horses. He would have been delighted with your brave decision to come out here and give Windarra a try.'

Kelly swallowed. A *try*! Hadn't Blade told Grace she had decided to stay here for good? *Why* hadn't he told her? Resentment rose in her throat. Because he didn't *want* her to stay and didn't expect her to stick it out for long. And Grace wouldn't want her to stay either. Naturally Blade's mother would want to see her own son settled at Windarra—so conveniently close to Bilba.

'I'm more than giving it a *try*, Mrs Ryan,' she corrected stiffly. 'I intend to stay, to keep it running for my father . . . to run it as well as he did.'

Grace Ryan regarded Kelly thoughtfully for a long moment. 'Maybe there's even more of your father in you than he thought,' she murmured at length. 'And, dear, please call me Grace.'

Kelly's taut muscles relaxed slightly, 'Would you—tell me about him?' she begged.

'I'll see if Biddy has our tea ready.' Excusing herself,

Megan vanished into the house, thoughtfully leaving them alone.

Grace sat back, sighing faintly. 'We didn't see Mungo often. He kept very much to himself. We tried to include him in our social activities; we asked him to Bilba often, but he rarely came. For a long time he was a lonely, bitter, disillusioned man. He lived for his horses—nothing else seemed to matter to him. He did become quite close to Blade though after Will, my husband, died. We saw a little more of him during that time.'

'Did he ever talk about my mother or—or me?' Kelly asked hesitantly.

Grace's soft brown eyes—Megan's eyes—were sympathetic. 'Not until these last few years. I think he always found it less painful to blot you both out of his mind—out of his life. It was only when he read in one of his horse magazines that Rowena Shaw's daughter had become a successful show-jumper that he began to show an interest. Until then I don't think he had actually thought of you as *his* daughter at all. It seemed to hit him then for the first time that you weren't just Rowena's child. You had *his* blood in your veins as well.'

'I wish he had let me *know* he felt that way,' Kelly said pensively. 'I would have tried to see him.'

'I think he was afraid to intrude on your life, dear—afraid of a rebuff perhaps. When he did finally make up his mind to contact you it was too late. He suffered his fatal heart-attack.' Grace's voice was filled with compassion—whether for Mungo or for Mungo's daughter, Kelly couldn't be sure.

'Yes,' was all she said, too choked up to say more.

Megan, bearing a trolley of freshly baked scones and tea, was a welcome diversion. After that they chatted about inconsequential things, and Kelly was warmed by their friendliness. Whether it was prompted by mere neighbourly courtesy or was a genuine offer of friendship didn't seem to matter so much anymore. They had broken the ice, that was the main thing. And the Ryan women were showing no sign of antagonism whatsoever.

After a while Kelly rose to her feet. 'Time I was heading back,' she said. There was a distinct chill in the air now and Grace must be feeling it.

Blade Ryan's towering figure emerged from the curtain of grapevines bordering the patio.

'Ah—I was just coming to drag you away. How you women do gossip! Come and say hello to Sherwin before you go, Kelly. You can pick up your mare from the stables.'

What choice did she have? It wasn't that she didn't want to see Sherwin—it was simply that Blade Ryan was making her feel ridiculously edgy these days—edgy and unsure of herself. If she didn't take care, it would start affecting her work—her judgement. But what was the point of trying to avoid him? As near neighbours, they would have to meet from time to time—and there were her flying lessons on Sundays; she didn't want to give up those. So pull yourself together, my girl, she thought, and act like the mature adult you've always prided yourself you are!

'It's been great meeting you, Grace.' She held out her hand.

Grace caught it in hers. 'I'm glad we've met at last too. You must come again, dear—just pop in any time. Now that the weather's growing warmer, you must drop in for a swim some time. Come over a bit earlier in the day—come for lunch. Any time.'

Kelly's heart swelled. 'Thanks, Grace—I will,' she heard herself promising. 'And I hope you'll be fully recovered very soon. I'd like you all to come to dinner at Windarra,' she said. 'Would you feel up to coming next Friday evening?'

Grace looked faintly surprised. 'Why, I'd love to come, dear—we all would, I'm sure. But it's such a busy time of year, and you have so much to——' Kelly thought she was going to say *learn*, but her actual words were 'keep up with'. Blade Ryan would have said 'learn', Kelly reflected ruefully. He must take after his father. He certainly hadn't inherited his mother's tact!

'No, please, I'd love to have you all,' she insisted. 'It won't be a four-star dinner, by any means—but we do have plenty of fresh beef and a good selection of home-grown vegetables. I'm afraid I haven't had a chance to do much about the house yet, though—my own things still haven't arrived from the States. The house still looks——' she hesitated, loyalty to her father making her think twice about going on.

'We've all seen the house, Kelly—don't worry about it,' Grace said swiftly. 'I can understand what you mean about wanting your own things. The place became very austere, very functional, after your mother left.'

Kelly gave her a smile, relieved that Grace understood why she wanted to introduce some changes. She was relieved too that Grace could talk about her mother without strain. Turning to Megan, she said, 'Thank you for the afternoon tea, Megan. I hope you'll feel free to come visit me at Windarra—any time. That you both will.'

Was she making a mistake? she paused to wonder. Falling into the Ryan trap? Inviting the enemy to call! Only Megan and her mother Grace didn't strike her as the 'enemy', they seemed totally removed from all the intrigue and the shrewd manoeuvrings that Blade Ryan was so proficient at.

Or was she being naïve? She mulled over the question as she swung round to follow Blade to the stables. Could Blade be using his mother and sister to soften her up? She wouldn't put it past him! Much as she wanted to accept their offer of friendship at face value, she knew she would be wise to be cautious, to hold back, just a little. People, as she had found out in the past, and more so since coming to Windarra Valley, could be mighty devious, and fiendishly clever, and no once could be cleverer than Blade Ryan! How did she knew the Ryan women weren't the same?

She kept these thoughts in mind as she accompanied Blade to the stables, as she peered into Sherwin's stall and uttered soft words of sympathy when she saw the dressing on his leg, and as she reached out to pat his velvety nose.

There was a young freckle-faced lad in the stall with Sherwin.

'Leo, what are you doing in here?' Blade asked with a

frown. 'Where's Mike?' Mike, Kelly recalled, was Sherwin's strapper.

'He's gone to have something to eat.' The lad's reply was rather defensive, almost surly. 'He said I could stay here with Sherwin. I've been grooming him.'

'You know that's Mike's job, Leo. You're supposed to be sweeping the paths. Off you go now.'

Tight-lipped, Leo slipped past them and fled.

Kelly glanced at Blade enquiringly. So, he was as autocratic here, as much in command, as he had shown he could be at Windarra!

'A bit full of himself, that one,' Blade muttered after Leo had gone. 'He only came to us on Friday—turned up out of the blue, begging for a job. Expected to be given horses to work with straight off. I said if he could show he was genuinely keen to work on a horse-stud by doing any odd jobs we asked him to do for the first couple of weeks, we'd think about keeping him on. He's only been here for three days and already he's bored with the odd jobs.'

'He seemed to be very good with Sherwin,' Kelly ventured. 'You can see he loves horses, and handles them well. He's probably just a bit over-keen, that's all.'

Blade shot her a look that made her wish she had shut up. Blade Ryan wouldn't relish being told what to do, she realised too late—especially on his own property. And by a woman!

'I'd better be going,' she said hastily. 'I want to get back before dark.'

'I'll ride back with you,' Blade said curtly. It wasn't a particularly gracious offer. He felt it his duty, no doubt!

'No, thanks,' she said, equally terse. She was remembering the way Blade had called out to her secretary Mary Lou, 'See you tonight, I'm looking forward to it.' No wonder he didn't want to ride her all the way home at this hour! Not when he was planning to spend his evening with Mary Lou! 'I'd rather ride alone,' she added, irritably aware that her spirits had taken a sudden nose-dive. 'I can think better when I'm alone.'

'And you have a lot to think about?' he murmured,

walking with her to her mare, already saddled and waiting.

'Haven't *you*?' she challenged. Let him think about how
well her afternoon had gone with his mother and sister—let
him worry about that! Because if he *hadn't* been deliberately using his womenfolk to disarm her—to make her
think more kindly towards a Ryan offer to buy her out—he
must be feeling vaguely uneasy about the way she and his
family had taken to one another. With such amiable
neighbours, why would she want to leave the valley!

Kelly had a full and busy week. As a result of Heathcote's
win in the Caulfield Cup, her phone had been ringing hot
ever since. People who had stayed away previously were
now wanting to come and see her, and bookings for mares
were pouring in. Confidence in Windarra Stud had been
restored, and people in the Australian horse-breeding
industry were making her feel warmly welcome in their
country. It's *my* country now, she thought happily.

On Friday evening Kelly waited apprehensively for her
guests to arrive, having checked and rechecked that
everything was in readiness, the dining-room table
immaculately set, the candles already alight, the wines
chilled, the salads prepared, the steaks marinated, ready to
throw on the fire at the last minute, and the stereo quietly
playing Mozart in the background. The fragrance of
jasmine, lilacs and roses filled the lounge and the dining-
room, and floating bowls of pale pink camellias flanked the
silver candelabra in the centre of the dining-room table, the
colour and beauty of the flowers, along with the indoor
plants she had introduced, bringing the two rooms to
vibrant life.

She moved nervously to the mirror over the fireplace for
a last check on her own appearance. She had chosen a
simple cream dress that flared into graceful folds from the
narrow gold belt at her waist. Her only jewellery was a gold
bracelet at her wrist and a single gold chain at her throat.
She had been careful not to dress too formally; she had a
feeling that the Ryan women wouldn't be ones to overdress
and they would feel uncomfortable if she did.

In the flickering candlelight her hair shone like polished black opal, her gently sun-tanned skin had a pearly translucence, and her violet eyes glimmered with a conspicuous glow. Seeing it, she pursed her lips. Was it a glow of anxiety, because the Ryans were visiting for the first time, because this was her first real dinner-party in her new home and she was anxious for it to go well? Or was it a glow of apprehension, because Blade Ryan was coming? If that were so, whom did she fear the most—Blade Ryan, the *man*, or Blade Ryan, the aspiring future owner of Windarra Stud? Either way, he was a formidable opponent, and she would need to keep her wits about her—especially here on her own home ground; the very ground *he* wanted to possess!

When the Ryans arrived, they walked in without Blade.

'Last-minute problems with a pregnant mare,' Megan explained with equanimity. 'He'll be along later in his own car. Dan wanted to stay too, but Blade and I talked him out of it. Truly, marrying a stud-man is going to be worse than being married to a doctor!' She looked teasingly at her fiancé as she spoke, denying the words with a fond smile.

Dan Cassidy was tall, lanky and deeply tanned, a quiet man with an easy-going air and a good-natured smile. Kelly at once felt she had summed him up accurately; he looked as agreeable as he had sounded on the phone.

Joe McQueen had also arrived, looking a vastly different man in his jaunty cravat and neatly pressed trousers; closely shaven for once, with his hair, so often hidden by a cap or a shady slouch hat, tonight slicked neatly back.

After assisting Grace Ryan into an armchair and waving Megan to another, Kelly began handing around the eye-catching *hors d'oeuvres* she had earlier prepared herself, while Joe saw to the drinks and Elsie Duncan buzzed about in the kitchen carrying out last-minute preparations for their three-course dinner of home-made leek and lentil soup, steak and salad, and Elsie's speciality, apple pie topped with fresh cream.

When Blade eventually arrived, he walked in with Mary Lou! Whether it was sheer coincidence, and they had merely driven up to the house at the same time, or whether they had arranged a private rendezvous first, Kelly refused to speculate. But she noticed that Mary Lou, as she moved across the room, had grass clippings clinging to her dainty high-heeled shoes, suggesting she had stepped off the gravel path outside on to the freshly mown lawn for some reason. Ridiculously—treacherously—Kelly had a vision of Mary Lou meeting Blade Ryan in the shelter of the shrubbery— the same shrubbery that had once screened *her* when she had collided with Blade Ryan on her way back to the house!

'Won't you sit down?' she invited, a bright smile concealing her skittering thoughts.

When they eventually moved into the dining-room, she sat herself at one end of the table and Blade at the far end between Megan and Mary Lou. Although she and Blade were facing each other, end to end, the tall candelabra in the centre of the table effectively masked him from her view—as she had known it would. Having him at a safe distance made her feel more comfortable. Let Mary Lou have him to herself, if that was what they both wanted!

The conversation over dinner was light and spirited, covering a range of topics, though invariably coming back to breeding and blood-lines and the coming Melbourne Cup. Mary Lou, Kelly noted, was her usual bubbly self— and judging by the way she was giggling and chatting with Blade, she was enjoying herself. The two, though, were not making their interest in each other too glaringly obvious. It would never do, Kelly thought caustically, to let Windarra's new boss see that her private secretary was romantically involved with the man who wanted to buy her out!

Just as Elsie was about to serve her mouth-watering apple pie, a phone-call came through from the stables, where Harry Watts was on duty for the evening. Harry wanted Joe to come and look at a mare that was about to give birth. As Joe excused himself and headed for the door, Blade rose too.

'Want me to come too?' he offered.

Joe waved him back. 'I'll ring from the stables if we need

you—thanks, Blade.'

They were half-way through their apple pie when the phone rang again. It was Joe, to tell Kelly they were going to need a vet. Did she want to call their regular vet, who could probably be there in twenty minutes, or would she ask Blade—'since he offered', Joe added diplomatically.

Kelly, appreciating the fact that Joe had deferred to her first, hesitated for only a second. If their own vet was slow in coming, it might be too late.

Blade, she noticed, was already on his feet. She nodded to him, and he acknowledged the nod with a brief salute as, peeling off his jacket and throwing it across the back of a chair, he strode across the room.

To Kelly's surprise, Mary Lou pushed back her chair and ran after him, her high heels clicking on the polished boards. 'Can I come with you—*please*, Blade? I don't see enough of what goes on in the stables during the foaling season, only being here in the daytime. I won't get in the way, I promise.'

Blade paused in the doorway. Despite the beseeching look in Mary Lou's big blue eyes, Kelly expected Blade to wave her back. She knew how he felt about a woman's rightful place; and Mary Lou was such a dainty, feminine creature, Kelly couldn't imagine Blade wanting the girl to witness a difficult birth, let alone allow the girl to risk soiling her pretty shoes and her flimsy pink dress.

She was stunned when Blade stood back with a resigned smile—a much softer smile than Kelly had ever seen directed at her—holding the door open for Mary Lou to pass through. All he said was, in a rueful tone, 'How will those shoes of yours go on the gravel?'

'Oh, never mind these.' Mary Lou smiled up at him as she slipped past him into the night.

'You'll find my boots on the veranda,' Kelly called after her, trying to convince herself she didn't care what Blade Ryan allowed Mary Lou to do. 'Slip into those, if you like.'

'Thanks. I will.'

The door slammed behind them. Kelly took a long deep breath before she turned back to face the others. She saw

Grace Ryan's eyes on her and hastened to explain away her rather bemused air.

'Mary Lou usually doesn't want to go anywhere near the stables,' she said with a laugh. 'She's got a real thing about it. I don't know why.'

'Oh, I do,' Megan put in. 'Your father told Blade all about it. Mary Lou had a bit of a fling a while back with your groom, Nico. It broke up when she discovered he was seeing another girl each Saturday when he was supposed to be visiting his parents. Apparently she's been avoiding Nico—and the stables—ever since. Nico, I gather, isn't on duty in the stables tonight.'

'No, he isn't,' Kelly said, wishing that Joe had told her about Mary Lou's break-up with Nico, rather than having to hear it from a neighbour—worse, a *Ryan*. Knowing Joe, even if he had thought of it, he wouldn't have considered it important enough to mention; Joe wasn't one for idle chit-chat.

'Guess it is a bit awkward for them,' Dan muttered. 'Working on the same stud-farm with a broken romance behind them. Embarrassing.'

Kelly nodded absently. And had Mary Lou now started a *new* romance? A romance with Blade Ryan? She wished her heart would stop leaping about the way it was. There was no need for it. Blade Ryan's caresses the other night had meant nothing—to him *or* to her. He was free to chase after Mary Lou or any other woman as far as she was concerned!

I won't think about it, she decided, nodding to Elsie to bring in the coffee. It's no business of mine, of no possible interest to me.

Why then did she feel so relieved when the two came back, barely half an hour later—and why so unutterably depressed when she saw the glowing radiance in Mary Lou's face? Had the safe arrival of a new foal put it there? Or had Blade Ryan? Kelly knew how potently attractive Blade could be to a woman. Only think of the advances he had made to *her*! But he had had an ulterior motive in her case. She mustn't forget that. 'We were both a bit emotional,' he had explained it away the next morning. But *she* knew better. It came back to Windarra Stud, every time!

In Mary Lou's case—sweet, feminine, vulnerable Mary Lou—could Blade Ryan possibly be *serious*? Mary Lou didn't strike Kelly as the kind of girl who played around. A girl who was so upset by a broken romance that she had shunned the stables ever since didn't sound like the kind of girl who was only out for a good time.

The words of the dark-eyed airline stewardess came leaping back. 'If he chooses anyone, he'll choose a fluffy, feminine little thing.'

A girl like Mary Lou? Would Blade Ryan be content with a girl like that? Kelly wondered dubiously—and resolutely dismissed them both from her mind.

As they were sipping their coffee the telephone rang again.

'It's for you, Blade.' Elsie looked worried. 'It's Bilba. They say it's urgent.'

Blade was on his feet and over to the phone in two long strides.

'Blade. Yes?' A short silence followed. '*What!*' You could have heard a pin drop in the room. 'Where is she? How long has she been there? Oh, my God, I'll be right there! Stay with her!'

Blade slammed the receiver down. When he turned round his face was like thunder.

'That damned new boy—Leo—left a gate open and Gretta wandered into the paddock he's been harrowing. She got tangled up in the chain harrow. Her leg's broken. It's bad. They think she's beyond help.'

Dan Cassidy sprang to his feet, his face blanching under his tan.

'What about her foal—and the other mares?'

'They're back in their own paddock—they're all right.' Blade already had his hand on the door. 'It's only Gretta, thank God. One of our best mares!' he added harshly. Only then did he seem to remember Kelly, to remember where he was. 'You'll have to excuse me——'

'I'll come with you.' Dan leapt after him, turning as he

reached the door. 'Megan, you've got your car. There's no need for you and Grace to leave yet.'

As Megan nodded, Kelly ran to the door. 'I'm so sorry,' she said to their retreating backs, but only Dan seemed to hear, smiling wanly as the darkness outside swallowed him. Of course, Kelly thought with a rueful sigh, wishing she didn't feel so helpless, so useless—this was man's work. The womenfolk were to stay at home and keep the home fires burning!

But that was unfair. She watched Blade's headlights spring on and saw the car leap forward as the engine coughed to life. Blade Ryan was a qualified veterinary surgeon, and it was a vet who was needed here. If the mare Gretta was truly beyond help, Blade had a grim task ahead.

She quailed for careless Leo who had left the gate open.

CHAPTER SEVEN

KELLY was in the stables early the next morning when a phone-call was put through from the house. It was Blade.

'I'm calling to thank you for last night—and to apologise for breaking up the party.' Before she could even ask after Gretta, he was drawling. 'You see how your social life tends to get disrupted when you live on a thoroughbred stud-farm?'

She stifled a sigh. 'You can't stop, can you? You'd love me to throw it all in, wouldn't you? Any minute now you'll be pointing out precisely what I'm missing—or what you *think* I'm missing.' If he only knew it, she had tolerated more often than enjoyed the endless round of dinners and parties and award evenings she had been obliged to attend on the show-jumping circuit.

'Not at all.' His answer was as smooth, as unruffled as always. 'I don't want to see you making a mistake, that's all.'

'Don't lose any sleep on my account,' she snapped. Then, remembering Gretta, she asked quickly, 'Did you manage to—to save your mare?'

'No.' A grim, taciturn *no*. 'Nothing could have saved her, even if I'd been on the spot in the first five minutes. Megan's going to have to feed her foal until it's old enough to wean.'

'Blade, I'm sorry—truly sorry.' Her anger was forgotten. She knew what the loss of a valuable mare meant. 'I guess that young lad—Leo—is devastated.'

She heard a sound the other end, a far from sympathetic sound. 'How he feels is immaterial. I've sent him packing.'

Kelly's teeth tugged at her lip. 'You don't think he'd have learned from such a tragic mistake?' she ventured. 'It wouldn't have been deliberate, just—just careless.'

'Closing gates after you is the first thing you learn on any stud-farm,' Blade said harshly. 'He's managed to kill one of our most valuable brood mares, and he could have killed a whole lot more, and their foals along with them.'

'But—Blade, that boy's crazy about horses—he's good with them too. Without a recommendation from you, he might never get another job on a horse-stud!' Kelly knew she shouldn't question Blade's decisions, but she couldn't hold the words back. Her heart went out to the boy. He was so young, so obviously keen to work with horses, and this, presumably, was his first serious mistake. Grave though it was, he must have learned from it.

'No second chances.' Blade's tone was implacable. 'He didn't give Gretta a second chance. A lad has to be willing to do any kind of work in this business, and do it to the best of his ability. I don't want any sloppy workers here.'

'I'm sorry it had to end the—the way it has,' Kelly said, thinking of Leo as much as the mare. Behind Blade's anger, she knew there must be pain, deep pain; and it would be that, as much as his anger, that was making him lash out at Leo. Poor careless Leo, who might have lost his chance to work again with horses. Word would quickly get around about his carelessness, and about his dismissal, and who would want to employ the lad then?

'Yes. Well, I've a busy day ahead,' Blade said tersely. 'I have to fly down to Sydney. See you in the morning. Flying lesson at ten sharp.'

He rang off before she could utter the words that sprang to her lips. *Why bother with flying lessons if you're so busy?*

She heaved a sigh as she replaced the receiver. Why *was* he persisting with their lessons? Why had he offered to teach her in the first place, when he clearly wished her a million miles away? She ran her fingers through her hair in a gesture of weary frustration. *Because he wants Windarra and he'll hang around you until he gets it!*

Well, Blade Ryan, she thought, tight-lipped, you'll have a long, long wait!

Later in the morning she had a surprise visitor. It was none other than the freckle-faced lad called Leo, who had left Bilba that morning in disgrace.

He was close to tears as he poured out his story.

'I never meant to do it, I swear I'll never do it again, I've learnt me lesson. Workin' with horses is all I ever wanted to do, but how will I get another job when people hear what I done? All I'm asking is for another chance—the chance to work for *you*, miss, so I can make good an' people will forget what I done.'

Kelly didn't answer at once. The lad did sound genuinely remorseful, and he was so very young—hardly out of school. He deserved a second chance. But if she took him on, Blade would be livid. He would think she was deliberately defying him.

She chewed on her lip. Would that be so terrible? For Blade Ryan to know that she could stand up to him, that she could withstand his possible wrath? If she did decide to take on the lad, she would have to tell Blade, of course—tell him before anyone else did. She wouldn't want him thinking she had taken the boy on behind his back. That wasn't her way. Whatever Blade thought of her decision, however angry he was, she would take his reaction squarely on the chin—and defend her decision to his face.

'I'll take you on on one condition,' she said to Leo. 'That you do a rather tedious job for me first—nothing to do with the stables. If you do it well, we'll consider a job in the stables.'

'I don't mind what I do, miss.' Leo's small dark eyes gleamed with relief. 'I'll do anythin'—anythin'! You're good, miss, real good. *He* wouldn't even give me a second chance,' he added plaintively.

She spoke to him sternly at that. 'If you are to stay here, Leo, I don't want to hear any criticism of the Ryans—do you understand? They had good reason for reacting the way they did. Rather than feeling bitter, I would prefer you to show them just what you are capable of.'

'Oh, I will, miss. I will, don't you worry.'

Something in his voice gave her a momentary qualm, but she dismissed it. The lad was anxious to show the Ryans they had been mistaken in dismissing him, that was all. He was anxious to make amends.

She set him to work clearing the tennis court, and while he was doing that she had a word with Joe McQueen about what she had done, and why. Joe did not look over-happy about her decision—was he thinking of Blade Ryan's reaction?—but he didn't question her judgement. He just 'hoped it would turn out all right'.

So do I, Kelly found herself thinking as she returned to the house to do some work in the office, since Mary Lou didn't work at weekends. The girl had already gone home after spending the night at Windarra.

She rang Bilba in the afternoon, but Blade wasn't back yet.

'Would you ask him to phone me the minute he gets back?' she asked Megan.

'Sure. Nothing wrong, I hope?'

'Oh no. Nothing. There's just something I want to tell him.'

'He should be back very soon. How about coming over for a cup of tea and a bite of the carrot cake I've just made?'

Kelly hesitated. It would certainly be less cowardly to tell Blade face to face, rather than over the telephone.

'Thanks, I will. See you shortly.'

As she changed out of her work-shirt and trousers into a clean white shirt and navy cord jeans, she looked out of her upstairs window in the direction of the tennis court, where young Leo was still hard at work. He had thrown himself with great gusto into the task she had set him, stopping only at lunch time when Kelly had taken him to the stables to meet the rest of the staff and to show him his quarters.

Before leaving the house she put a call through to Joe, asking him to send one of the lads to keep a discreet eye on Leo, and in an hour or so to let the boy stop work for the day.

She enjoyed a pleasant afternoon tea with Grace and Megan, and when Blade still hadn't arrived home, Megan suggested going down to the stables to see Sherwin, who, she remarked, looking pleased, was making a remarkable recovery from his injury.

'Won't be long, Mother,' she said, touching Grace's shoulder. 'Call Biddy if you want anything.'

'I'll be fine, dear. I think I'll take a nap,' Grace said, waving them off.

Today there was a thin layer of cloud covering the sky,

but it was more wispy than threatening. The sun above was a glary blur.

'Mike's just taken Sherwin for a dip in the river,' one of the lads told them as they strolled into the stables.

'Never mind,' Megan said. 'I'll show you around, Kelly, while we're waiting for them to come back.'

A short while later the drone of a light plane overhead signalled Blade's return. Kelly's heart began to thump nervously. She felt like rushing back to the house, jumping into her car, and driving out to the airstrip to meet him, simply to get her guilty confession off her chest.

'Ah, here comes Sherwin now,' said Megan, and Kelly forgot about Blade and Leo in the pleasure of seeing Sherwin again, showing no sign of lameness now, his stride long and free and easy, his every movement fluid and confident.

'I'm so glad he's all right,' she said sincerely, stroking his silky nose while Mike rubbed him down, the horse's rich red coat still damp from his swim.

'Blade, Kelly wants to see you about something. You walk her back to the house while I stay here and help Dan for a while. Mother's having a rest.'

Kelly swallowed hard as she fell into step beside Blade. She didn't want to see that warmth fade from his eyes, but she knew it would, the moment she told him what she had done.

She was right.

'You've *what*?'

'I've taken Leo on. I thought he deserved a second chance.' She held her head high, secretly flinching at the anger in his eyes.

'Lads like Leo don't deserve a second chance. There's a streak in that boy I don't like—never did. It wasn't just the laziness—it's something I could never quite put my finger on. A look about him. I should never have taken him on in the first place.'

'Isn't that rather unfair? Just because you don't like a lad's looks? Leo can't help the way he looks. Is it his close-set eyes you object to?' she demanded with heavy sarcasm. 'Or is it his freckles that bother you? Or his pinched little face?'

'It's more than that——'

'But you can't say *what*,' she challenged. 'He's awfully young, Blade; he can't be long out of school. I admire his spirit—coming to me for a job when he knows I'm a close neighbour and a friend of the Ryans. He was quite frank about what he had done—and he was truly sorry, Blade. It *was* his first and only mistake, wasn't it?'

'A pretty costly one, wouldn't you say? He made it plain that ordinary farm work was beneath him. That was the whole trouble. He didn't take care because he didn't like what he was doing.'

'I'm sure he's learnt his lesson,' she said quietly, determined not to lose her own temper. 'He's quite happy working on the tennis court. He's a good worker, Blade.'

'Well, I wish you luck.'

'Thank you,' They had reached the paved brick courtyard where she had left her car. 'I'd better be going. I . . . just came over to let you know what I had done.'

He looked at her for a moment, his eyelids flickering. 'Thank you. I appreciate that.' He planted his hands on his hips. 'If I were you,' he said, 'I'd keep an eye on him all the same.'

Blade Ryan, always having the last word, always so convinced that he was right and she was wrong!

She turned her back on him and stalked to her car.

At ten fifteen the next morning she was wondering where Blade was. He was normally so punctual. Five minutes later he arrived—on horseback. To her surprise, she saw he was leading Sherwin alongside.

'He was ready for a good long walk.' Blade said, springing nimbly from the saddle. 'Tomorrow he'll be resuming light training—which is all he'll need before he races again. We're running him in the MacKinnon Stakes on Saturday down in Melbourne—it's considered a good lead-up race to the Melbourne Cup on Tuesday.'

'I don't think Heathcote is racing on Saturday,' said Kelly.

'I know. I guess your trainer felt he didn't need it. Sherwin does, after his enforced spell from racing.'

Leaving both Sherwin and Blade's black gelding in the capable hands of Harry Watts, Kelly and Blade strolled back to the house together, neither mentioning young Leo, who was hard at work on the tennis court behind the house.

'Today we'll study some theory—on *terra firma*,' Blade said, patting a slim briefcase he had brought with him.

'Let's go into the office,' Kelly suggested. 'I'll clear the desk.'

For the next couple of hours they pored over charts and diagrams and weather maps, with only the occasional phone-call interrupting them—save a more welcome diversion when Elsie brought them a tray of lemon tea and buttered jubilee cake, fresh out of the oven.

Kelly was grateful to Blade for what he was doing, for giving up his time to teach her, but she wished she could have been surer of his motives. Would he regret these lessons one day, when she was still here, and he had to look for some other place to buy?

'Will you stay for lunch?' she asked when he finally packed up his papers.

'Sorry. Must get back. We've some people calling in.'

Knowing it would take him a while to ride back, she made no attempt to detain him. Her stomach dipped when, returning to the stables with him, she saw young Leo standing alongside Sherwin. Blade's big gelding was grazing nearby.

'Where's Harry?' she asked sharply, looking around. She was conscious of Blade directly behind her, saying nothing.

'He's just popped off to fetch something.' The freckles stood out starkly on the lad's pinched nose. 'I said I'd mind Sherwin till he got back.' He stomped off, muttering, 'I'll saddle the gelding for you.'

'I thought the boy was working on the tennis court—not in the stables.' Blade's voice grated in Kelly's ear.

She swung round to face him. 'It's Leo's lunch-break. His lunch time is his own, Blade. If he wants to spend the time here in the stables getting to know the horses or lending a hand, why should I object to that? Treat people fairly and I believe they will treat *you* fairly.'

'And you think I wasn't fair, you don't have to spell it

out. Well, let's hope you don't burn your pretty fingers!'

When the boy came back with the saddled gelding, Blade took the reins from him without comment.

'Sherwin's better, is he?' the lad asked, running his hand along the chestnut's glossy neck.

'Quite better, thanks,' Blade answered curtly.

'So he'll be racing on Saturday? And in the Melbourne Cup Tuesday?'

'All being well.'

'Well, good luck,' said the lad, ambling away. 'I got to get back to work.'

'Cheeky young devil.' Blade glared after him.

'Cheeky?' Kelly echoed. 'Plucky, I'd say. Standing up to the formidable Blade Ryan.'

'He's not even sorry for what he did.' Blade hissed the words through his teeth. 'Not one word of remorse.'

'I guess he tried saying he was sorry before you kicked him out,' Kelly said sweetly. 'Even a boy in the wrong has his pride.'

A reluctant smile tugged at Blade's lips. 'He certainly has a champion in you, hasn't he? Do you often take up lost causes?'

'I don't consider Leo a lost cause. He's a good worker. He's given me no reason to regret taking him on. You saw him with Sherwin just now. You can see he loves horses.'

'I loved Gretta.' Blade mounted the gelding in one fluid movement and swinging the horse round, led Sherwin out of the yard without a backward glance.

Grace Ryan phoned the next day with an invitation to dinner. 'Does Wednesday night suit you?' she asked.

'Oh, Grace, that would be lovely, but—are you sure you feel up to it?'

'Perfectly sure, dear. Besides, we have a special reason for getting together. It's a celebration. The entire Bilba staff will be coming, and we want you to be here with us.'

Kelly stopped breathing. A celebration? Why did she suddenly feel the room tilting? Celebrating *what*? Not . . . not an engagement!

Blade's engagement? His engagement to . . . She swallowed. To Mary Lou?

Dear God, could those two actually have fallen in love? Actually be planning to get married?

Kelly had the sick feeling she was tumbling into a gaping black void—a new and frightening sensation. She had never felt this way before in her life: aching, desolate, numbed. She didn't understand it. It made no sense. Why should Blade Ryan's engagement to Mary Lou—to anyone!—matter a jot to her? What was Blade Ryan to her?

A deep convulsive shudder ran through her. No. Her hand flew to her lips. Not *that*! It was unthinkable. It was crazy. She couldn't be falling in love with him herself!

Her heart rolled over. No, *hardly*. They were bitter enemies. They couldn't agree on anything. He didn't even want her to stay in the valley! And yet—and yet there were times when——

She groaned aloud.

'What is it, dear?' Grace's question brought her back to earth with a painful jolt.

She gulped. 'I'm—I'm intrigued, Grace.' Was that her own voice answering? It sounded disembodied, unfamiliar, as if it belonged to somebody else. She sighed, grasping at normality. Where was the famed Kelly Nagle Heath composure? She opened her lips again. 'Grace—um, you mentioned a special reason.'

'It's a farewell celebration, dear—for Sherwin. A good luck celebration.' Kelly's head spun—a *farewell* celebration! 'He'll be going back to Melbourne at dawn the next morning. Kelly dear, we'd like to make it a joint occasion— for you and Heathcote as well. One of us has to lose the Cup, I know—maybe both—but think how wonderful if one of us happened to win! Bilba's first Melbourne Cup! Yours too, dear. Not Windarra's first, I know—but *your* first.'

Kelly's relief was so overwhelming that she burst into giggles, something she couldn't recall doing since her high-school days. She tried to explain them away.

'Oh Grace, the thought of it! I—I feel so darned excited! I've barely had time to think about the Melbourne Cup. I'd love to come for the evening. What a great idea!'

'It will be an informal affair, dear—a barbecue. Weather permitting, we'll have it on the patio by the pool— otherwise inside the house. Would you like someone to come and pick you up, to save you having to drive home afterwards?'

'Oh, no, thanks, Grace—I'll drive myself.'

'Look, why don't you throw in a nightie and toothbrush and stay the night? Come around eight, dear. We'll look forward to it.'

'Grace, thank you. So will I.'

Kelly felt nervous; she didn't know why. Who was she kidding? It was the thought of coming face to face with Blade Ryan again, now that she knew, now that she had realised . . .

She chewed on her lip. That she loved him? Doubt flooded through her. She couldn't be in love with him—not with Blade Ryan! It was madness. It was laughable, impossible, illogical, it made no sense! A one-sided love, a *futile* love! She almost laughed aloud at the absurdity of it— only she had an uneasy feeling that her laughter would dissolve into hysterical tears if she gave way to it.

She pushed her silky black hair behind her ears and fastened a pair of small gold earrings, examining their effect in her bedroom mirror. Too demure, too prim. Her dangling gold earrings, she decided, would look better, complementing her embroidered cream wool blouse and her tan suede and leather skirt with its fringed leather pockets. *Informal*, Grace had said. A *barbecue*.

Boots? Or shoes? She decided on her brown suede boots. And a three-cornered leather scarf to match her skirt at her throat.

As she drove to Bilba alone, her banished thoughts crept insidiously back. Truly, it was ironic! To think that she, Kelly Nagle Heath, who could have had her pick of an endless string of eligible admirers—among them the debonair, strikingly handsome, world-renowned show-jumper, Harvey Quinn—had fallen for the one man she could never have—the one man who would never want *her*. He might have lusted after her *body* once or twice, but love had been the last thing on Blade Ryan's mind, let alone marriage and a life together. It was Windarra Stud he wanted—not her.

Kelly heaved a sigh. As her car bounced over the uneven road she pictured his face as she had last seen it, tight with disapproval because she had defied him over the lad called Leo, taking the boy on against his express advice. What did she see in a man who was dictatorial and hard-hearted and scheming and inconsiderate? Had she gone crazy?

She deliberately closed her mind to the electrifying effect his kisses had on her, to the way she had mindlessly responded to his touch. They were feelings that weren't to be trusted! Just as *he* was not to be trusted! She closed her mind just as firmly to his good points, his undoubted competence, his brilliant mind, his glowing achievements, his regard for his horses and his family. They, too, would only cloud the issue. The man was ruthless and ambitious and he wanted Windarra Stud—*that* was what she had to remember.

When she arrived at Bilba, the evening was already in full swing, the stable staff obviously relishing their night off and the prospect of a slap-up feed. Someone had strung coloured lights around the pool, and the staff were mingling with the family on the patio. Kelly glanced up at the sky as she headed for one of the outdoor tables, where she could see Grace Ryan flitting about. The evening was unusually warm—ominously warm. The sky had been heavily overcast all day, and Kelly knew that Grace must have been watching the gathering clouds with foreboding.

When she voiced her thoughts aloud, Grace merely laughed.

'If it starts to rain we'll just move inside. The barbecue itself is under cover, that's the main thing. We can eat indoors if we have to. We won't be dismayed to see some rain—we need it badly. I don't think it's rained since——'

'Since the day Kelly arrived,' a voice said from behind.

Kelly's heartbeat quickened as she turned her head and looked up into Blade Ryan's shadowed face, his tawny hair glowing blue, red and gold under the coloured lights.

'Excuse me, dears,' Grace said, slipping away. 'I must see to the salads.'

'Can't I help?' Kelly pleaded, twisting round, but Grace shook her head, thanked her with a smile, and vanished into the kitchen. Kelly might have followed regardless if Blade's hand hadn't closed over her arm.

'Mother has enough helpers. Come and meet the lads. We call them all "lads", both male and female—it's easier. I suppose that offends your feminist sensibilities?'

'Not at all,' she answered coolly. 'I think it shows a gratifyingly non-chauvinist outlook—treating them all equally, male and female. I commend you,' she mocked. 'I didn't think you were so broad-minded where women were concerned.'

'Then you still have a lot to learn about me, haven't you?' His head was bowed over hers, his eyes like smouldering coals in the soft, dancing light, his lips tormentingly close.

She tried to back away and found she couldn't. 'Would you kindly let go of my arm?' she demanded shakily.

Instead of complying, he swung her round with a soft chuckle and bore her across to the nearest group of guests. Only then did he release her, drifting off to fetch a round of drinks.

She relaxed then, though she could still feel the imprint of his fingers on her arm. She remained conscious of his touch—and headily aware of his nearness, even when they were apart—even as she mingled and chatted and laughed with first one group, then another. It was a pleasant evening, spiced with an underlying excitement—the excitement of knowing that Bilba's champion, Sherwin, was fit and ready to return to Melbourne the next day to prepare for his run in Tuesday's Melbourne Cup.

The Ryans hadn't forgotten Heathcote either, and both the family and the Bilba staff were generous in wishing Kelly luck too. There was some good-natured teasing, and a fair bit of leg-pulling over the friendly rivalry between the two neighbouring studs, but Kelly, who was beginning to understand and appreciate the notorious Aussie humour, took it all with a smile.

Later Blade Ryan came and claimed her for a dance. As his arms swallowed her, her cheek came into contact with the silk of his shirt, warmed by the heat of his body, and she stifled a sigh. Soft music drifted across the patio and swirled around them as they danced, while above, the twinkling coloured lights lent an air of unreality and romance. A distant roll of thunder added a vague sense of danger and expectancy.

They moved in unison, their bodies moulded together, swaying as one. Despite her brave thoughts, for a few dizzying moments Kelly forgot the harsh realities of life and gave herself up to the dream. If only it could always be like this—the two of them moving in perfect harmony—pulling together instead of pulling each other apart! Would it ever happen? She doubted it. Certainly not until Blade Ryan gave up wanting Windarra Stud—and that he would never do.

She sighed. No, Blade Ryan would never give up. He still expected her to toss it all in and walk out—the way her mother had. He had always looked on her, damn him, with doubting, cynical eyes, with the same cynicism with which he appeared to look on all women save his own immediate family—and a fluffy young country girl called Mary Lou!

Blade merely smiled, secretly incensing her further. 'Want to come to the stables and wish Sherwin good luck?'

She nodded before she stopped to consider it. 'Sure.' Only when she had committed herself did she suffer a qualm. Visiting the lonely stables at night with Blade Ryan, with this air of excitement and danger about, and her emotions tossing her this way and that and her head still a bit fuzzy from the champagne she had consumed . . . wouldn't she be playing with fire?

She cast about for a belated excuse. 'If it rains, I——' she looked down at her leather skirt and suede boots.

'Megan will lend you an oilskin and gumboots or whatever,' Blade was looking past her now—trying to catch Megan's eye.

'Oh, no, I——' but it was too late; Blade was already beckoning Megan over.

Within minutes she was on her way to the stables with

Blade, her leather skirt discarded in favour of a pair of jeans belonging to Megan, her feet swimming inside Megan's gumboots, and with a yellow oilskin thrown over her shoulders, just in case.

The stables, lit this evening by only an odd light or two, looked shadowy and deserted. There was an eerie, almost breathless silence hanging over the yard. The calm before the storm? Kelly wondered, looking up at the low sooty clouds.

As if in answer, a blinding flash illuminated the sky. Seconds later a deep ominous rumble rolled across the valley.

'We'll look in on the foaling-paddock first,' Blade said, catching her hand. 'We've had no one there keeping a direct watch tonight, though if any foals were on the way, the alarm would have sounded. We switched it through to the house.'

There were only two deep-bellied mares in the foaling-paddock tonight. Blade switched on the powerful foaling-lights and after a brief, thorough inspection of both mares, he declared with certainty that neither would give birth for at least twenty-four hours.

'Come over here, I'll show you how to tell.' He beckoned Kelly closer. Under the bright lights he demonstrated with a few simple, deft movements how to tell when a mare was close to giving birth.

'Here—examine her yourself,' Blade invited, standing back.

'Joe has already shown me, thanks,' Kelly admitted, frowning slightly. She didn't trust the glint in his eye. 'If you were hoping I'd be squeamish about doing that sort of thing, forget it. It doesn't bother me a bit.'

'You're a remarkable lady, Kelly Heath,' he said with a quick grin.

She caught her breath at his use of her name. *Kelly Heath*, he had called her. It had always been Kelly *Nagle* Heath before. Was it a step towards acceptance, or was that too much to hope for?

Their eyes met for an instant. The silence seemed to close in on them, heavy and oppressive—and potent.

'Let's go and see Sherwin before that storm hits,' Blade suggested, diffusing the sudden charge atmosphere between them.

'Let's,' she agreed readily, in a slightly choked voice.

There was a young girl curled up on the straw in Sherwin's stall. Kelly remembered meeting her earlier in the house.

'Mike said he'll be here to relieve you in about half an hour, Jenny,' Blade said as the girl scrambled to her feet. 'He'll be bedding down here with Sherwin for the night—they want to make an early start in the morning. The rest of you can play on for a while yet.' He smiled at the girl, and Kelly marvelled at the spontaneity, the sincerity of his smile. Did he reserve the mockery and the cynicism for ex-show-jumping heiresses?

'How is Sherwin?' she asked Jenny, not wanting to proceed with that train of thought.

'A bit restless.' The girl's hair was close-cropped like a boy's, and she spoke with a marked Australian twang. 'He senses there's a storm coming. Not that it's likely to worry him that much, as long as he's snug in his stall. Hey——' her head shot round. 'Did you hear something?'

As she voiced the question, a clap of thunder rocketed overhead, shuddering away in eerie echoes, sounding as if a dozen giants were stampeding across the sky, shaking sheets of galvanised iron as they went.

'Better make a dash for the house,' Blade advised. 'We might just beat the rain.'

As they hurried from the stable, jagged lightning zigzagged across the sky and a bomb-like blast of thunder sent Kelly jumping almost into Blade's arms.

'Better run! Keep away from the trees,' Blade yelled, throwing his arm round her to steer her forward. 'And pull that hood over your head.'

Kelly was quick to comply, having learned on her first day in Australia how rapidly a torrential downpour could drench the unwary. Blade, she noticed as she ran, had no covering for his head, and the collar of his waterproof jacket did little to protect his head or neck. Half-way to the

house the rain started, pouring down with a thunderous
roar, soaking Blade's bare head in seconds. The path at
their feet was ankle-deep and streaming with water well
before they reached the shelter of the verandah.

Out of the rain at last, and breathless, their damp faces
aglow and eyes glistening, they both looked at one another
and burst out laughing.

'So that's what a drowned rat looks like!' Kelly gasped,
choking back her laughter.

'Huddled in that wet raincoat and hood, you look like
something out of *The Wind in the Willows*,' Blade responded
with a chuckle. He reached up and pushed back her
dripping hood. Then he proceeded, with deliberate care, to
unbutton her oilskin coat. Their eyes met in the pool of
light thrown by the lantern above them. She saw the
laughter fade from his eyes and a new expression take its
place, and she felt a quiver run through her. Her lips parted
involuntarily and her tongue flicked out nervously to
moisten them. Was it merely desire she was seeing in his
eyes, or something more tender? If only she knew!

Their eyes remained locked together as his fingers
continued their task, eventually pealing the dripping
oilskin from her shoulders and letting it drop to the
flagstones at their feet. Then he pulled of his own jacket,
discarding it as he had hers, his eyes never wavering from
her face.

'Kelly.' His voice was hoarse as his damp fingers closed
on her shoulders, cool through the soft wool of her blouse.
'Come here.'

She knew he was going to kiss her. She wanted to stop
him, knowing how vulnerable she was now and still unsure
whether she could trust him or believe in that tender look in
his eye; suspecting that he was simply responding to the
headiness of the moment, that to him she was no more than
an attractive, desirable woman who possessed something he
wanted for himself. Windarrra Stud.

But her body refused to obey her, wouldn't allow her to
pull away. As his lips touched hers, she stood mesmerised,
numb with a longing that, much as she wanted to deny it, to
fight it, overpowered her will.

His mouth on hers was moist from the rain, his kiss tantalisingly sensual, sending a rush of heat through her yielding body. Trickles of cool water ran from his wet hair down the furrows of his cheeks to mingle with their moving lips, as her own mouth responded under his.

Feeling her response, his kiss deepened, sending waves of emotion pulsating through her. She felt his hand move down her body to rest on the swell of her breast. Trembling, her body strained closer, her hands going up and around his neck. He made a husky sound of pleasure against her lips, and it was all she could do to stop herself crying aloud, 'Oh, Blade, I love you!' but, tempting as it was to believe that he might love her too, she still had a shred of pride left, enough to keep her silent. She was thinking of Harvey Quinn and other men before Harvey who had pursued her, men who had blurted out too quickly their love for her, arousing in her a vague sense of contempt for their weakness, knowing her own heart to be untouched. She couldn't afford to show any such weakness now, in Blade Ryan's arms, though it was becoming more difficult by the second to control the powerful emotions that rocked her. One day, if she didn't pull herself together, she would stop trying altogether. And then Blade Ryan would have her at his mercy!

She realised that he had drawn back his head and was watching her, his eyes slate-grey pools that seemed to be peering into her deepest soul. How much did they see? she wondered uneasily, becoming still in his arms.

'You seem to have something on your mind,' he said, his hand still stroking her breast, sending steamy pulses through her, even as her body stiffened at his words. Blade Ryan was an alarmingly perceptive man, a fact she couldn't afford to forget. He didn't miss a thing. Now was the time to pull away, before she was well and truly lost.

Her arms slid from his neck and at once his own, instead of tightening around her, dropped away. She saw wariness shimmer in his gaze.

'We'd better go back and join the party,' he said, his voice impassive now, giving her no clue to his real feelings. She let her breath out in a shallow sigh, relieved that she hadn't tumbled any deeper into the enticing pit he had been drawing her into, doubly thankful that she hadn't uttered the damning words that had trembled on her lips. Getting involved in any way at all with Blade Ryan was playing with fire—she could end up badly hurt if she didn't take care. Fortunately, Blade had made no secret of what he was really after. And painful though it was, she had a fair idea, too, where his true feelings lay—at Mary Lou's daintily shod feet. Which made his caresses just now empty and meaningless. Knowing that helped to arm her against him.

Mary Lou, for her part, was being almost pathetically tolerant and patient, Kelly reflected, pursing her lips. And extremely broad-minded as well, if she had any inkling of what had been going on behind her back! No doubt both she and Blade thought that the end justified whatever means were required, and that a little pain and inconvenience now would be all worth while once they had achieved what they were after, Windarra Stud.

Little do they know what they're up against, Kelly rallied, ignoring a painful twinge in the region of her heart as she bent to pull off Megan's gumboots. I have been a fighter all my life—and a winner too. I don't intend to give in to the first man who succeeds in challenging me at my own level. Even if I do damned well love him!

CHAPTER EIGHT

ONCE inside, they went their own ways, Kelly hurrying off
in search of Megan, or Grace, or anybody, Blade vanishing
through a doorway in search of a dry towel. It wasn't until
at least twenty minutes later, while she was dancing with
Dan Cassidy in Bilba's long hall, the party having moved
inside as soon as the rain started, that she spied Blade's
neatly combed head above the heads of Megan and Jenny,
the girl who had been in the stables earlier with Sherwin.
Other groups had spilled into the adjoining rooms, where
they were sitting or standing around, chatting, listening to
music, or dancing in any available space. Distant thunder
could still be heard, and the rain was still falling steadily,
drumming on the iron roof.

A head appeared over Dan's shoulder.

'G'night, mate. I'm going down to the stables now to
relieve Jenny. I'll be bedding down there for the night.'

Kelly recognised Sherwin's young strapper, the red-
headed Mike.

'But Jenny's already here,' she said, her eyes flicking
across the room. Her gaze met Blade's, a fraction of a
second before Blade caught sight of Mike. Kelly saw him
look down at Jenny, frown, then grab the girl's arm and
yank her across the room.

'If you're both here,' Blade said harshly, *'who is with
Sherwin?'*

'You were meant to stay with Sherwin, Jenny, until
Mike came,' Dan put in, his tone, though milder than
Blade's, no less condemnatory.

'I did stay—Mike *did* come——' Jenny protested.

'What are you on about?' Mike broke in. 'I haven't left
the house all night! I've got the last shift, remember? I was
just coming now.'

Blood suffused Jenny's face. 'But you came and banged

147

on the stable door! I heard you shout to me to go back to the
house. When I made a dash for it through the rain, I saw
you over by the tack-room, Mike. You waved to me and
yelled at me to run.'

'That wasn't me,' Mike burst out, his own face by now as
red as Jenny's.

'Your voice was a bit muffled by the rain,' Jenny
admitted, 'and I couldn't see you clearly.' She screwed up
her lips. 'You were wearing a grey raincoat with a hood.'

'It wasn't me,' Mike repeated stonily. They looked at one
another, and then, in sudden fear, at Blade.

'Oh, hell,' was all that Blade said, and the three men,
with Jenny at their heels, made a dive for the door, pausing
only long enough to pull on gumboots and oilskins before
plunging out into the thudding rain. Kelly stumbled after
them, snatching up an oilskin on the way. Thinking that
Megan might want her gumboots to come after them, she
didn't pause to look for another pair, rushing out in her
fashionable suede boots, which she had pulled on over
Megan's jeans. She barely noticed the rain beating down on
her head, or the deep puddles as she ran, her heart sinking,
Blade's grim expression still vivid in her mind. Why would
someone pretend to be Mike and send Jenny back to the
house unless—unless——

Their worst fears were realised when they found the door
of Sherwin's stall hanging open, banging eerily against the
stable wall.

'He's gone! Sherwin's *gone!*' howled Mike, his face
contorting with agony. He wheeled on Jenny, clutching at
a dim hope. 'You must have left the door open! And now
he's bolted in fright!'

'I didn't leave the door open! I shut it securely—and I
remember pushing the bolt across,' Jenny vowed. 'It must
have been that—that person I saw. The one pretending to
be you, Mike!'

Dan darted into the building and the next moment the
stables were ablaze with lights.

'Start looking!' Blade rasped. 'Search the yard first! If
Sherwin's bolted in this storm, he could have run straight

into a fence—or into a hole, a tree—anything!'

Kelly had a vision of Sherwin's precious legs, of his beautiful body lying badly injured, somewhere out there in the dripping darkness.

A frantic search of the yard and the immediate environs revealed nothing, and the rain had obliterated any tracks which might have given a clue to the direction Sherwin had taken.

'Put a call through to the house!' Blade commanded Jenny as they regrouped in the yard. 'We'll need all the help we can get.' He was saddling one of the horses as he spoke.

'He's either bolted off down the road—down *one* of the roads—or he's been *led* away,' Dan said in a taut voice.

Blade said grimly, 'Who the hell would——' and then he stopped. His eyes met Kelly's, and she flinched at the cold fury she saw there. He rapped at her, 'Go and phone Windarra! Tell Joe to alert your lads to watch out for a bolting horse—or a strange van—anything unusual. And check on that boy you took in!'

She felt a sick numbness sweep over her. Dear God, let Leo be there, she thought. If *he* had let Sherwin out—or worse, had led him away, with goodness knows what in mind... She closed her mind to the unthinkable consequences; consequences that could affect both Bilba and Windarra.

Within minutes she was back with the bad news.

'Leo is missing,' she told Blade dully. 'And one of our stock-horses is missing as well. You were right about him, Blade—I should have listened to you.'

'Yes, by God, you should have!' She had never seen Blade so blazingly angry. 'Just wait until I get my hands on the brat! If he's hurt Sherwin I'll break his good-for-nothing neck!' He turned to rap a command at Megan, who had come running along with the stable-hands, in response to Jenny's call. 'Megan, telephone the police. That boy Leo is behind this. He's either turned Sherwin loose—or he's led him away. Ask for road-blocks—the boy won't get far if he has Sherwin with him. Get them to stop every truck and van in case he had an accomplice waiting.'

He swung back to face Kelly, his eyes glinting coldy under the harsh stable-lights—a look that chilled her to the bone. 'Describe your horse!'

'He's a bay gelding with white markings on his rear legs and a white blaze on his nose,' Kelly answered promptly. As Megan ran to the phone, she asked Blade tentatively, 'You—you think someone else might be in this with Leo? Someone with a *truck*?'

'Who knows?' Blade was looking at her, Kelly thought miserably, as if he hated her. Or was her guilt magnifying his totally justifiable anger? 'If it *is* a conspiracy, heaven forbid, let's hope it's only money they're after, and that they're not out to inflict some injury on Sherwin—or *worse.*'

Dan broke in. 'If they meant to harm Sherwin or——' he hesitated '—do away with him, you'd think they would have done it here on the spot, not taken the risk of being caught with him. The boy's probably just led him away and let him loose somewhere as a petty revenge on us for kicking him out.'

'In this weather, that could be just as fatal as putting a bullet in his head,' Blade said harshly. He jerked his head round to rap orders at his men, who grabbed flashlights, rifles and mounts and rode off into the soggy darkness. As Blade swung into the saddle to join the searchers, Kelly darted forward, turning her face upward, oblivious of the rain that was plastering her black hair to her head, ignoring the cold droplets that were trickling down her neck.

'Let me come with you, Blade!' she begged. 'Give me a mount so that I can join in the search too.'

Blade regarded her as though she were an irritating insect buzzing round his legs.

'Afraid I'll throttle your young protegé when I find him?' he asked nastily.

'No, Blade! I want to help you find Sherwin!'

'Don't you think you've caused enough trouble already? Stay here with the women and leave the searching to the men.'

Kelly planted herself directly in his path. 'If you don't give me a horse, I'll drive back to Windarra and get one of my own,' she threatened. 'Maybe I should do just that,' she added as a thought struck her. 'I might catch sight of Sherwin on the road.'

'You might damned well run over him too! You're not driving a car in this weather. Anyway, Dan and his boys are riding out that way now. And Joe and your lads will be covering the road from your end. Stay here and give the women a hand. Be ready with coffee and dry clothes—the men will need them. Or stand by the phone. There's plenty to do right here.'

'And plenty of women to do it! I want to come with you,' she repeated doggedly, not moving.

He looked as if he wanted to strike her. 'You heard me! You're to stay here. Do as I say. *For once!*'

Her chin rose a notch higher. 'I would have thought you'd be grateful for an extra hand. Isn't Sherwin worth every bit of help you can get?'

'Damn it, Kelly, why do you always have to be so hellishly pig-headed? You don't hear Megan insisting on riding out with the men—she knows where she is the most valuable. Right here, at home!' He heaved a exasperated sigh. 'Why can't you be like other women?'

'You have preconceived, totally archaic ideas about what a woman should be,' Kelly flung back. 'Why should your men be any more capable of searching for the horse than I am? Look, I'm joining the search whatever you say! The women don't need me—but *you* do. Are you going to give me a horse or do I have to drive home to get one?'

When he didn't answer at once, she appealed to him. 'Blade, I feel responsible, don't you see? Taking Leo on was a big mistake—I admit it. But he sounded so damned plausible. I truly believed he wanted to make amends.'

Blade said grudgingly, 'You weren't to know what was in the little swine's mind.' She sensed a backing down, and pressed home her advantage.

'Then you'll let me come with you?'

He looked down at her for a long moment. Then with a

shrug, he yelled out to Megan to saddle up another horse. 'Come with me then!' His voice grated at Kelly. 'And stay close. I don't want you haring off on your own. There's no way I'd trust you with a gun!'

'I'm perfectly capable of handling a gun,' she retorted, hiding her long-standing aversion to firearms. 'It's only a matter of firing a shot into the air, isn't it?'

'A shot? It could just as easily be three shots!' Blade brutally pointed out, and she felt a tiny shiver run through her as she recalled the men's prearranged signal: one gunshot to mean simply 'Come home'; two shots to mean that Sherwin, or his trail, had been found; three shots to signal that help was needed—pronto! 'And you know what that could mean.' Blade's face hardened. 'If Sherwin is badly hurt, what follows might not be a pretty sight.'

Kelly said a silent prayer for Sherwin—and for Blade too. She was thinking of the night Blade's mare Gretta had been injured as a result of Leo's carelessness, and the grim task Blade had had to face as a result. It couldn't be happening again! That would be too cruel.

Blade eyed her frostily. 'Still want to come?'

'Yes.'

'Then let's go.'

She moved out of Blade's path at last and mounted the brown mare Megan had saddled for her, swinging her round to follow Blade into the wet, swirling darkness.

Conditions could not have been much worse. Though the worst of the storm had by now passed over, the rain was still drumming down, the roads had turned to slush, and in the darkness it was possible to miss seeing something almost under their noses. Though both she and Blade had powerful flashlights, the rain and the darkness diffused their beams of light, bringing visibility down to a few metres. Progress was painfully slow. Every tree, every stump, every dark hollow could hide a clue, or worse. At the same time they had to watch their footing, never sure if a puddle lying in their path was deep or shallow, whether the grassy verge alongside was safe or dangerously slippery, whether the mud underfoot was going to bog them down.

Blade had brought a walkie-talkie radio with him, to maintain contact with Megan back at the stables. If the police phoned Bilba with news, they would hear straight away. It remained ominously silent, however. As they ploughed on, squinting against the steady rain, with a cold dampness seeping into their bones, no longed-for messages came, and no rifle-shots rang out to signal either good or bad news.

'Don't go wandering off on your own!' Blade cautioned roughly as they reached the sloping, heavily wooded gully. 'If you get lost, don't expect me to waste time looking for you. Sherwin's my first priority. Just keep me in sight—or at least stay within shouting distance. And be careful! I have enough problems without anything happening to you!'

'I'll be careful,' Kelly promised, her heart torn by the ragged anguish in Blade's voice, which even his anger couldn't hide. She could understand his concern—and his frustration. They weren't even sure what they were looking for—a single runaway racehorse, or a young lad riding one horse and leading another. Or even a gang of horse thieves!

Surely, she thought despairingly, as time ticked by without a sign or a clue, Sherwin couldn't possibly be wandering alone out here in this hazardous, dark, dripping world? Would the boy Leo, who had struck her as a true horse-lover, have callously abandoned a valuable race-horse, even one belonging to Blade Ryan, in these appalling conditions? Or even worse, was he even now smuggling Sherwin away in a truck, to some fate that didn't bear thinking of?

'I told you the life out here wasn't for the faint-hearted,' Blade reminded her, noting the despondent slump of her shoulders. 'Thinking of packing it all in?'

'Why should I?' she snapped, stung that he could still think that she might.

'You gave your show-jumping away. And I imagine that was a lot easier and more profitable than your life out here.'

'You still don't know me, do you?' she muttered, and swung her mare away so that she wouldn't have to listen to any more—so that he couldn't see the sudden tears that sprang to her eyes.

They rode in silence after that. At times they heard distant shouts from the other searchers, but there were no resulting gunshots, and no messages came through on Blade's radio. All the searchers had specific areas to cover, some scouring the valley floor, others following the roads and the rapidly swelling river, the rest, like Blade and Kelly, skirting the heavily timbered side gullies.

An hour dragged by, and then another, before Kelly heard Blade give a shout. She rode over to join him as Megan's voice crackled over his radio.

'Blade, the police have found Kelly's gelding—at a farm just outside Wattlefield. The lad has stolen a motor-bike from the same farm. They've lost him, I'm afraid. No one stopped him at the Wattlefield road-block—they were watching out for horses and vans, not bikes or cars. Blade, the boy rode into the farm without Sherwin—he must have abandoned him before he reached the farm—most likely before he even left the valley! The police are sure he didn't transfer Sherwin to a van or anything—no suspicious trucks have been sighted anywhere in the area.'

Blade's jaw tightened. 'Then where *is* he? We've been searching for hours and there's no sign of him. If the little wretch simply let Sherwin loose, you'd think we would have found him by now.'

Megan's voice crackled back. 'Blade, the police are maintaining their road-blocks and they have other men working their way back along the road between Wattlefield and Bilba Valley. Will I recall our lads and get them to concentrate on that corner of the valley?'

'Yes. Please. I'll work my way round following the gully—though I'm a bit baffled. Mike and his group will have searched round there already. Where the hell can Sherwin be?'

Kelly knew what he was thinking. If Sherwin was alive and well, surely they would have found him by now.

'Keep looking, Blade.' Megan's voice, distorted as it was, had a comforting ring. 'We'll find him. And that boy too.

I'll go and fire off a shot to bring back the others. I'll have hot drinks ready and dry clothes—and spare horses if they need them. Is Kelly still with you?'

'Yes, but I'm sending her back.'

'No!' Kelly burst out. 'Blade, *why*?'

'You two fight it out.' Megan's voice sounded mildly amused. 'Bye now. Good luck!'

'Blade, I'm staying,' Kelly said firmly.

'Don't be a fool. You look half frozen and half drowned,' Blade said, running his eyes over her bedraggled form. 'And just look at your hands.'

Kelly looked down. Her hands were almost blue. And yes, they did feel quite numb with cold, it occurred to her now. And it was only then that she became aware that the legs of her jeans—*Megan's* jeans—were wet through and spattered with mud, clinging damply, coldly, to her thighs. The suede boots, she knew, would be ruined. As for her hair, she could feel it sticking in wet spikes to her face, and she knew she must look pale, pinched, and wobegone.

'I'm fine,' she insisted. 'And I'm not going back. You need me now more than ever—the others will take a while to get here.'

'I don't want you falling off your horse with exhaustion,' Blade said, his voice anything but warm.

She sighed. He saw her as an encumbrance. He was afraid she would collapse on him—either from cold or fatigue—and he would have to look after her.

'I've ridden in worse conditions than these,' she assured him, deliberately straightening in the saddle and putting on a brighter face.

They heard a shot ring out, its report echoing across the valley. Though muffled by distance, it was still clearly audible. Megan's signal.

'Well, come on then,' Blade said impatiently. He was obviously too concerned about Sherwin to argue any further. He would never have given in so easily otherwise. In normal circumstances, Blade Ryan never gave in— certainly not to a woman! 'At least we know what we're looking for now,' Blade added grimly. 'Not two horses and a boy, but one stray racehorse.'

What they didn't know—and neither voiced aloud the fears they felt—was in what condition they would find Sherwin.

For the first time it struck Kelly forcibly how the situation could affect *her*—or more particularly her livelihood at Windarra Stud. Sherwin and her own horse Heathcote were close rivals for Tuesday's Melbourne Cup—Australia's richest, most prestigious race. If it leaked out, as it was bound to do with the police already involved, that a Windarra Stud employee had spirited Sherwin away, she, Kelly, would be blamed by a lot of people. And she would have no real defence. She had employed the lad against Blade Ryan's express wishes. It would look as though she and the boy had plotted this shoddy affair together—Leo seeking revenge, she seeking to rid herself of a dangerous rival!

If Sherwin fails to turn up safe and well, she vowed silently, I'll scratch Heathcote from the Melbourne Cup. It's the least I can do to show people I care about Sherwin, and that I'm not out to win at any price. She tightened her lips resolutely. Regardless of what people might say or think if she did leave Heathcote in the race, she knew she wouldn't want to win at Sherwin's expense.

The first pearly streaks of dawn were beginning to appear in the sky, and the rain had lightened to a floaty, irritating drizzle. Kelly heard a muttered oath from Blade and tugged her mare round to fall into step beside him.

'Have you seen something?'

'No,' he growled. 'Nothing. That's just it—there's *nothing*. Where the hell can Sherwin be? If the boy let him loose in the valley—around here somewhere, on his way to Wattlefield—why haven't we found him? We've looked everywhere!' His eyes fluttered upward. 'He's hardly likely to have wandered up into the mountains. They're too steep.'

Kelly gave a quick intake of breath. 'I've just thought of something.'

'What?' Blade said sharply.

'What if Sherwin was *led* up into the mountains,' Kelly said slowly. 'Do you recall me telling you about Leo borrowing a horse yesterday and going for a ride? He mentioned vaguely that he'd been *up to the mountains*. I assumed he meant the mountains behind Windarra. But what if he rode into Bilba Valley and explored the mountains behind *Bilba*—looking for a place to hide Sherwin?'

Blade didn't waste time on questions or recriminations. Kelly could see his mind leaping ahead, considering the possibility.

'There are a number of caves up in these mountains,' he said at length, stroking his chin. 'The largest one—Leo might have heard about it from the other lads when he worked at Bilba—is Black Jack's Cave. Bushrangers used it once as a hideout. We often used to ride up there as kids. You'd better stay down here—it's pretty rugged, and after all this rain it could be dangerous.'

'Please, Blade, let me come with you,' she pleaded. 'If only for moral support.'

She didn't know why she had said that—it had simply popped out. Saying such a dumb thing to Blade Ryan of all people! As if the self-contained master of Bilba Stud needed any moral support—least of all from a woman!

Blade was looking at her in an odd way. Afraid that he was going to utter some derisive retort, she added quickly, 'Haven't I proved to you yet that I'm as capable as any of your men?'

A faint smile crossed his face at that, a smile totally free of mockery.

'I admit you've been far from a liability,' he conceded. 'It's been quite a comfort, in fact, to have you along. You haven't complained once. Even my men would have complained at least once.'

She smiled back involuntarily. 'Women have to do things better than men before they are noticed,' she returned without rancour.

Again she was conscious of his appraising look.

'I wouldn't think there has ever been a time when you

weren't noticed, Kelly Heath,' he drawled enigmatically. She wasn't sure if it was meant as criticism or as a compliment. 'I'll let Megan know where we're going,' he said, pulling out his radio.

'Be careful,' Megan's voice cautioned when she heard where they were going.

'Don't expect too much,' Blade advised her. 'It's a long shot; but it's worth a try.'

It was a slow, difficult climb up to Black Jack's Cave. At one stage they had to dismount and lead their mounts, picking their way between rocks and over dangerously slippery patches. Both had fallen silent, neither really believing they would find Sherwin up here, certainly neither daring to believe they would find him hail and hearty. It was simply another place to look. As Blade had said to Megan, it was a 'long shot'.

A fallen branch from a gumtree lay across the dark mouth of the cave. Seeing it, they glanced at one another, wondering if it had fallen there during the storm—or had been dragged across by human hand. By the look of it, the branch had not been there long—the leaves were still green and fresh. Neither spoke as they hauled it aside, both heaving together.

They heard a sound from inside the cave. A scuffling sound, followed by a muffled snort.

'Sherwin!'

Blade leapt into the cavernous darkness.

Kelly pressed her hands to her breast, hardly daring to breathe. She didn't follow Blade into the cave, waiting at the entrance in a fever of suspense. If Sherwin was hurt— badly hurt—she sensed that Blade would not want her to witness his initial reaction—he would want to control himself before facing her again.

'Kelly—come here!'

Her heart leapt upward. She could tell by Blade's tone that nothing was seriously wrong. Relief, joy, throbbed through his voice.

'He's—he's all right?' As she ran into the cave, Blade moved forward to meet her. He was leading Sherwin.

'Oh, Blade—Blade!' She was too choked up to speak.

Without letting go of Sherwin, Blade reached out his free hand and pulled her to him. His kiss was one of relief rather than passion.

'Thank God you remembered Leo riding up into the mountains—we might not have thought of looking up here for hours. I hope he hasn't caught a cold. Let's get him out into the light so I can examine him properly.'

The drizzle had stopped at last and the sky was ablaze now with red and gold streaks, casting an eerie orange flush over the limestone rocks and across the plain down below. As Blade ran his hands over Sherwin's body and down his legs, Kelly stood watching, biting her lip to hide her own emotion. The horse was still wearing the blue rug she recalled him wearing in his stall, but now it was almost black with damp. His normally glossy coat was dank and mud-spattered, but other than being wet, the racehorse looked none the worse for his ordeal.

'At least he's had water to drink.' Blade remarked gruffly. 'There was fresh water in a rock pool inside the cave. And the young scoundrel thought to leave some grass for him.'

'What's that on his collar?' Kelly said suddenly. 'It looks like a note.' She plucked a small folded sheet of paper from the horse's head-collar.

Blade frowned. 'Read it to me,' he said, squatting down on his haunches to run his hands over Sherwin's recently healed injury.

With a pounding heart, Kelly unfolded the note and started to read.

'"So now I've had my revenge and I'm satisfied",' she began, and paused, chewing her lip.

'Go on,' Blade said stonily.

She cleared her throat. '"I hope you been feeling real bad, Blade Ryan, and didn't find him too quick. I never meant Sherwin no harm, just to shake him up a bit so you'd have to scratch him from the Cup. Too bad if he gets a cold or a cough and is out for the rest of the season. He'll get over it, but you might not! You know why I done it. You never gave me a chance. But *she* did, even knowing what I done".'

Kelly swallowed, realising the lad was referring to her. She read on. '"You could say I done this for her, to give her horse a better chance to win the Cup."' She broke of with a disgusted snort. 'As if I'd want to win that way!'

'Anything else?' Blade said grimly.

She nodded, fighting down a wave of emotion. '"Don't try to find me. I'm leaving the State. I'll use a new name if I have to. Best of bad luck for Cup day!"' She couldn't look at Blade. 'It's signed "You know who".'

'Little blighter—when they find him I'll tear him limb from limb.' Blade straightened with a sigh. 'Well, Sherwin will certainly be missing Saturday's race—and he needed that run. Even if we could get him down to Melbourne in time, I wouldn't risk it. He'll need a good rest after this, and close watching for a day or two. That means the Cup on Tuesday is doubtful too. He'd have to be fully recovered by Saturday for the drive down to Melbourne. And missing Saturday's lead-up race means he'll have to go into the Cup cold, without a conditioning run. It won't be easy.'

'Oh, Blade, I——'

'Don't say anything.' Blade's hand touched her shoulder. 'I know how you feel.'

'But, Blade, you *can't* know! It's not only Sherwin I'm thinking of—it's the part *I* played in all this! I should have listened to you and sent Leo packing. I'm largely to blame.'

Blade's eyebrows shot up. 'For not heeding my advice?' he asked, and added teasingly, 'I find it hard to picture the aggressively independent Miss Heath taking any notice of that high-handed devil Blade Ryan!'

She flushed. 'Blade, I didn't take Leo on to be contrary— to thumb my nose at *you*. I honestly believed he deserved a second chance.'

'The lad was hell-bent on revenge, regardless.' Blade's voice sobered. 'He would have come back to Bilba whether you'd taken him on or not.'

'It wouldn't have been so easy for him, coming from further away.' Her argument was silenced by the touch of his finger on her lips.

'Hush. Now hold Sherwin for a moment while I go behind those rocks and fire a shot in the air. The men can go home now—I'll let Megan know.'

Home. How sweet the word sounded.

After firing off a single shot and giving Megan the happy news over the radio, Blade led Sherwin down the mountainside, Kelly and her mare following. Remounting in the gully below, Kelly faced Blade with a look of resolution.

'I'm scratching Heathcote from the Melbourne Cup,' she told him.

'You're *what*?' He looked genuinely nonplussed. '*Why*, for heaven's sake?'

She hesitated. How could she explain, without sounding trite or self-pitying? How could she tell Blade that if she ran Heathcote in the Cup, and especially if her horse won, *she* could end up the loser? The doubt in people's minds would always be there. *Did Kelly Heath conspire with that young horse-thief Leo to ruin Sherwin's chance of winning the Melbourne Cup?* People would shun her; *owners* would shun her. She, who had enough against her already! She was a newcomer to racing and breeding, a foreigner, and to many people she was the daughter of a fickle American movie star who had walked out on her Australian husband—and on Australia.

'I've made up my mind,' she said firmly.

'Don't be a fool,' Blade said with a harshness that startled her. 'How would it look if you scratched Heathcote now? As an admission of guilt! It would look as if you felt you had to *atone* for what you had done!'

Kelly's jaw dropped. 'Oh, my God,' she whispered. She hadn't looked at it that way. 'What can I do?'

'You can marry me.'

'*What!*' She almost fell off her mare. She looked at him sharply. 'This is no time for sick jokes, Blade Ryan.'

'It's no joke,' he said calmly. 'Marry me and no one will dare say a word against you. We'll announce our engagement right away.'

'You'd marry me to save my name?' she asked in

confusion. 'Or,' her eyes narrowed, 'to save Windarra's good name?'

'No, damn it! I *want* to marry you. I'm merely choosing now to ask you because I don't want you suffering from that boy's petty revenge on *me*.'

Could she believe him? Could she believe that he genuinely *wanted* to marry her? Blade Ryan, as she well knew, was a diabolically clever man—he always had a good reason for everything he did.

She took refuge in sarcasm. 'So it's a matter of honour. Very magnanimous, Mr Ryan. Well, I don't need any melodramatic gestures, least of all marriage proposals, thanks! I'd rather swallow whatever medicine I'm forced to swallow!'

'My, you're a stubborn woman,' he said mildly. 'You'd rather risk losing Windarra? You could, you know, if people decide they won't send their mares to Windarra any more.'

Cold logic was warring with her tangled emotions.

'And of course, if I were to ruin Windarra's good name,' she said slowly, eyeing him accusingly, 'you'd have an uphill battle restoring it.'

He looked as if he would like to take her across his knee and spank her. 'You're twisting things around to suit your pretty, musguided self.'

'I don't think so!'

'Kelly, is the thought of marrying me so terrible?' There was a new note in his voice, and the look in his eyes had changed imperceptibly too, in a way that confused her more than ever.

She looked away. It was hard to think clearly when he was looking at her in that way. If he only knew how tempted she was to say 'Yes, I'll marry you!' She drew in a long breath, her chest heaving as she vacillated, not knowing what to do, or what to say. If she agreed, would he learn to love her in time?

Cold reality washed over her. What a hope! It was more likely he would quietly break off the engagement as soon as this awful affair had blown over and been forgotten, and

Windarra Stud was secure again.

On the other hand, if she turned him down now, she could end up losing her beloved Windarra Stud! She could end up losing both Windarra *and* Blade, the two things she loved most in the world!

She didn't intend to lose both!

'All right,' she agreed hoarsely. 'I'll marry you.'

He didn't ask her if she meant it, if she wanted to reconsider; he didn't bounce for joy either, or draw her into his arms. He merely said, briskly, 'The announcement will be in the newspapers by the weekend—well before Melbourne Cup day. Whether Sherwin runs or not.'

She nodded, feeling numbed. Stunned. She had a mental image of Mary Lou, the way she had looked the night she and Blade had come back from the stables together, the night the Ryans had come to dinner. She wanted to ask Blade about the girl, but the questions stuck in her throat. If Blade really cared for Mary Lou, he would never admit it now. She wondered how he would explain his engagement to Mary Lou. *It's only a temporary thing, sweetheart, purely a business arrangement—a smokescreen to save Windarra's good name. It doesn't mean a thing. The wedding will never take place.* Or even, *We only have to be patient, my darling. Kelly won't want to stay here for ever. When she gives up on Windarra, the place will fall into our hands.*

Oh dear God, what had she agreed to?

CHAPTER NINE

KELLY went through the motions in a daze, flying down to Sydney the following day with Blade to choose an engagement ring, picking out a delicate solitaire diamond—the ring she would have chosen had it been a real engagement—and at Blade's insistence, buying a new outfit for the Melbourne Cup, a pleated white skirt and pale grey silk jacket with a narrow black tie, and as a finishing touch, a wide-brimmed white hat.

Blade's brother Ambler flew back to Bilba with them. As Sherwin's trainer, Ambler wanted to satisfy himself that his precious charge hadn't suffered any irreparable harm from his hours of shock and exposure. Even though Sherwin appeared to be recovering well, they all knew that even without any evident after-effects, the big red had a formidable combination of obstacles to overcome.

The Ryan family and Kelly's own staff at Windarra were ecstatic at the news of her engagement to Blade. She wondered if the Ryans' joy was a sign that they genuinely liked her, or was simply relief that Blade was at last going to realise his ambition to become owner, if only joint-owner, of Windarra Stud.

Blade deftly side-stepped any direct questions about a wedding date. 'We'll think about that after the Cup' was all he would say. Their engagement party, too, was postponed until after the big race. Everything just now was revolving around the Melbourne Cup. To Kelly, it was a relief that there was something else to think about. It gave her a chance to get quietly used to the idea that she had actually agreed to marry Blade Ryan. Even though she loved him and knew that she always would, she was under no illusions that he returned her love.

It was a frantically busy few days, everyone at Bilba and Windarra working feverishly to complete their chores

ahead of time where possible so that they could take time off
to attend the Cup. On Saturday Sherwin was pronounced
fit enough to travel, and his young strapper Mike
accompanied him in the horse-float when it set off for
Melbourne at dawn. Ambler had already flown back to
Melbourne, having satisfied himself that he wouldn't need
to scratch Sherwin from the Melbourne Cup, as he had
been forced to do from Saturday's race—failing anything
unforeseen happening, such as a last-minute cough
developing.

As for the cause of all the trouble, of Leo there was no
sign. It was as if he had vanished from the face of the earth.
No one really cared; they had Sherwin back safe and
sound, and the big race was now only a couple of days
away. That was what was filling their minds just now, not
the vengeful Leo.

When Mary Lou arrived at Windarra for work on
Monday morning, she already knew about Kelly's engagement to Blade. Kelly wondered bleakly if Blade had let her
know. Who else? If he truly cared for Mary Lou, Blade
would have wanted to break the news to her himself. Mary
Lou's congratulatory speech sounded convincing; her smile
appeared equally genuine. Carefully rehearsed, no doubt,
Kelly reflected painfully. At the same time she couldn't
help feeling a bit sorry for the girl. Even though Mary Lou
must be aware that it was only a mock engagement, it must
be hurtful for her all the same. Would Blade have sensed
that? Kelly wondered. She doubted it. Making a martyr of
his women would appeal to a male chauvinist like Blade
Ryan!

Casting Blade as the villain helped her to steel herself
against him—and against her own heart. No matter how
desperately she wanted to believe that her engagement was
real, she must not fall into that trap. When Windarra was
secure—when the publicity over Sherwin had died down—
she would release Blade from his promise to marry her—
before *he* could ask to be set free. And she would let him
know that he and Mary Lou would have to look for another

place to buy, because she intended to stay at Windarra—
for good!

Blade did not come near Windarra until early evening.
Had he been waiting for Mary Lou to leave, or had he
simply been busy all day, with the Cup looming tomorrow?
She couldn't bring herself to ask.

'You look a bit pale.' Blade looked at her closely. 'You're
not having second thoughts, are you?'

'Second thoughts?'

'About marrying me.'

'N-no,' she said unsteadily.

'That doesn't sound very convincing. What's wrong?'

'Nothing's wrong. I appreciate what you're doing for
me.' Damn it, that wasn't what she had meant to say!

'What I'm——' he broke off, swearing under his breath.
'Didn't I make it clear that I intended marrying you no
matter what? The incident with Sherwin only hurried
things along. I had planned to woo you first, that's all—to
give you a bit more time—before popping the question.'
His thumb-tip was gently rubbing her bare arm as he
spoke, his touch having its usual treacherous effect on her,
setting her nerve-ends tingling. She took a deep breath and
caught the faint scent of his cologne, spicy and masculine.

'You really *want* to marry me?' she asked huskily. She
heard, to her dismay, the yearning in her voice—how
piteous she sounded!—but that was what Blade Ryan had
done to her. She was no longer the self-sufficient Kelly
Nagle Heath who had always maintained the upper hand
with any man who crossed her path. Blade Ryan had
reduced her to a feeble shell of her former self!

'I wouldn't have asked if I hadn't meant it.' His fingers
were gliding up her arm now, feathering across her
shoulder, threading through her hair. With his other hand
he tilted her head upwards, and she felt a smothered
sensation as she looked into his face and saw the feverish
brilliance in his eyes.

'Blade——' his name was wrung from her lips, but no
further words came.

'Kelly,' he responded throatily, his face blurring as his

head came down, his lips seeking hers.

She closed her eyes and moaned, feeling the tension draining out of her as he twisted her mouth under his own and drank deeply from it. Her hands shook as they moved upwards of their own volition and clung round his neck.

With his mouth still firmly on hers, Blade gathered her in his arms and carried her across the room in the direction of the stairs. Kelly whimpered softly, her body limp and yielding, no longer wanting to fight, wanting only to drown in his arms.

He raised his head to mutter, 'You wonder if I really mean to marry you? I'm going to show you precisely how much I do mean it.'

His voice had changed; it was harsh now, roughened by a note of savage aggression that caused Kelly to stiffen uneasily in his arms. She stifled a ragged sigh. Where was the tenderness she yearned to hear, the blazing love she longed to see in his eyes? Was it only lust he felt for her? Was even that feigned, to get what he wanted?

All her old doubts swept back. Blade Ryan was a ruthless, ambitious man—he would do anything to get hold of Windarra Stud, even offer to marry a girl he didn't love, even make love to her first to convince her he was serious!

'No!' she cried, twisting out of his arms, forcing him to release her. 'You don't have to prove anything to me, Blade. Please, let's—let's wait.'

'Wait until our wedding-night?' Blade's eyes were mocking, but there was a glint of something else that puzzled her—and faintly chilled her. What was it? Frustration? Annoyance? Relief, even? Or something else? 'Of course, if that's what you want,' he agreed impassively.

It isn't, her heart cried, but her lips answered primly, 'Thank you, Blade. Anyway,' she seized on a diversion, anything to defuse the charged atmosphere between them, 'Joe will be here any minute. He wants to settle arrangements for tomorrow.'

'Ah yes, tomorrow. The Melbourne Cup, our Armageddon.' Blade's lip quirked, his eyebrows rising fractionally. 'Your Heathcote and our Sherwin.' He spread his hands.

'Well, it's in the lap of the Gods now, or it will be tomorrow.'

'Our Armageddon?' she echoed, frowning. 'You make us sound like deadly rivals, Blade, locked in the final battle!'

'Mm. I take it back. There's no rivalry between Bilba and Windarra, you have a ring to prove it.' There was a nuance in his voice that caused her heart to constrict. Was he still upset that she had pushed him away?

'Blade,' she bit her lip. 'Do you honestly think people will believe I had nothing to do with what happened to Sherwin?'

His hand closed on her arm. This time there was nothing provocative about it—it was simply a gesture of comfort.

'Nobody will dare say a word against you when you arrive at Flemington with me tomorrow—as my fiancée. You've no need to worry.' Though his expression was still aloof, giving nothing away, his tone was milder now.

The buzz of the doorbell, signalling Joe's arrival, was a welcome intrusion.

'I want Kelly to fly down to Melbourne with me,' Blade told Joe without preamble. 'Dan and Megan will be coming with us. Mother's decided to stay at home and watch the Cup on television. It won't be so tiring for her.'

Joe stroked his chin, dark with stubble after his long day's work. 'In that case I'll have room for Mary Lou in the Cherokee.'

'Good. Fine,' said Blade, making Kelly wonder with a pang if he would have offered to take Mary Lou himself if Joe hadn't had a spare seat.

'I'm taking Harry Watts and Elsie too,' Joe added, and Kelly nodded. She had already offered Elsie the day off.

'Who's going to be in charge here?' she asked Joe.

'Young Nico. He'll be all right—you can rely on Nico. He might be a bit wild where the ladies are concerned, but he's a good stud-man.'

Nico, the muscular young man who had once been involved with Mary Lou—until she found out he had been seeing another girl behind her back! Kelly grew thoughtful. It must have been upsetting for Mary Lou at the time.

Was that when Blade had first started seeing Mary Lou? Had he been consoling the young secretary, and their relationship had gradually grown into——

She preferred not to think about it. Wherever Blade Ryan's true emotions lay, he had promised to marry *her*, Kelly. Surely that meant he had decided to give up Mary Lou? Windarra Stud would come first to Blade Ryan, she suspected pensively—before any woman!

A light sprinkling of rain overnight had settled the track and the famous Flemington racecourse, bathed now in gentle sunshine, was looking magnificent, the lawns velvety in their emerald green freshness, the flower-beds abloom with pink, red, white and gold roses and a profusion of pansies, stocks, cinerarias and ranunculi.

The excitement round the packed lawns and stands was at fever-pitch. For the time being the champagne corks had stopped popping, the bands had stopped playing, and the photographers had stopped snapping. All eyes were on the barrier, where the horses were lining up for the start.

'They're off!'

The shout burst from Megan. Kelly caught her breath as the horses leapt forward in a line of glossy coats, flying hooves, and gleaming silks.

'Sherwin's *last*!' Megan groaned as the field thundered past the members' stand.

'He has a clear run though,' Dan said anxiously. 'He likes being an outside runner, remember?'

'Early days yet.' Blade's voice was unworried. It was a long race. It was seldom that the horses leading early were able to hold their pace for the full distance. Anything could happen. Already, Kelly noticed, straining on tiptoe, the two horses in the lead were falling back, and three or four others, in a huddle, swept past them, the rest straggling behind, looking for a clear run, or holding back until it was time to make their run.

'Heathcote's coming up on the rails,' squealed Megan, nudging Kelly. 'He's in a great position!'

Kelly nodded, hugging herself with excitement.

'Sherwin's starting to make up ground!' Dan shouted.

'Oh, *yes*!' Megan cried. 'Come on, boy, come *on*!'

Kelly heard herself shouting along with them. 'Come on, Heathcote! Come on, Sherwin!' Would Sherwin's lack of racing condition put him out of the running? He was still so far back in the field, it would take a miracle!

'Heathcote's got himself fenced in on the rails!' The shout burst from Blade, binoculars clamped to his eyes. 'Bring him *round*!' he urged the jockey. 'If you can't find a way through, go wide!'

Kelly held her breath, echoing Blade's words without a sound coming out.

'He can't!' Dan muttered. 'He *can't* get round! That damned grey's in his way, and *he* can't get a run either. There are four, five, all in a bunch!'

'Oh, what bad luck.' Megan's hand pressed Kelly's arm, before her gaze flickered back along the field. 'Where's Sherwin? I can't see him!'

Blade swung the binoculars round. 'There he is, coming up wide.' His voice was a deep rumble above Kelly's right shoulder. 'He's running brilliantly.'

But Sherwin was still well behind the leaders, still well back in the field, Kelly saw as she tugged her eyes away from Heathcote. Sherwin's wide barrier position and lack of race practice appeared to be defeating him, just as Heathcote's crowding on the rails was defeating *him*. It would take a miracle for either of them to catch the leaders now, with the field already nearing the home turn.

She heard Dan growl, 'Sherwin's too far back, he'll never do it—not from there.'

And Blade's voice, tight with tension, 'He likes to come from behind, and he loves a tight finish. He'll be trying his heart out.'

As the field swept round the turn and thundered down the home straight, Kelly gave a cry.

'Heathcote's found a way through! Come on, boy, come *on*!'

'It's too late.' Blade rested a comforting hand on her

shoulder. 'He's lost too much ground. They're almost home.'

She nodded, sighing, knowing it was true; Heathcote had lost his chance. Even now his path was not clear; he had to weave a corkscrew pattern to pass the horses still in front.

A tremendous roar rose from the crowd as the field pounded down the straight, silks billowing, whips flying. A fierce battle was being waged between the three horses in the lead, who were all bunched together, practically neck and neck, the rest of the field stretched out behind.

'Spearhead's going to win it,' Dan said glumly. 'He's got his nose in front.'

Kelly plucked her gaze away from the hapless Heathcote, who was still fighting gamely, already making up ground; but she could see that he was too far back in the field now to be a threat.

'*Look at Sherwin!*' Megan's shriek burst out over the roar of the crowd. 'Just look at him fly!'

Blade's breath hissed out in a gasp. Kelly stopped breathing altogether, gaping in disbelief. The big red was flying up on the outside, streaking past horse after horse. Only metres from the finish, he drew level with the leader, Spearhead.

'Come *on*, Sherwin!' Kelly shouted, forgetting Heathcote. You can do it! Come *on*, boy!'

'Sherwin! Sherwin!' chanted the frenzied crowd, dazed and delighted.

In half a dozen strides, Sherwin passed the finishing-post, a full length clear of Spearhead. Heathcote, fighting to the finish, came in a game fourth.

'He's won! Sherwin's *won*!' With a squeal, Kelly pivoted round and threw herself into Blade's arms. 'Oh, Blade! I'm so happy for you!'

Blade smiled down at her. 'I do believe you are,' he said, and pressed his lips to hers in full view of the cheering crowd.

He didn't release her straight away, his mouth lingering on hers until she felt herself responding, a smouldering weakness invading her limbs, filling them with liquid fire. There was warmth and tenderness and a throbbing passion in his kiss that made her want to cry out, 'Blade, Blade, don't kiss me like this unless you mean it!' but she couldn't utter a sound because his mouth was still firmly imprisoning hers.

'Blade, you'd better go down and lead Sherwin in.' It was Megan's voice, faintly amused, her fingers plucking them apart.

Blade lifted her head. 'Mm, yes.' Kelly found herself set free at last. 'You'd better follow me down,' he told Megan. 'You'll be needed for the presentation—you're a part-owner, remember? And, Kelly——' she melted at the tenderness in his eyes—was it only the euphoria of the moment that had put it there? 'I want you to be there too. Dan, look after them both, will you?' He shot off.

After the presentation, countless people, mostly strangers to Kelly, along with the press and TV cameras, crowded round the Ryan family. Blade kept Kelly firmly by his side, as though she were already one of the family.

Among their well-wishers were the party from Windarra Stud—Joe McQueen and Elsie Duncan, both hardly recognisable in their Cup-day finery, Mary Lou looking glamorous in a navy wide-brimmed hat and a navy silk coat over a red and white dress, and blue-eyed Harry Watts, also spruced up for the occasion.

When Mary Lou stood on tiptoe to give Blade a congratulatory kiss, Kelly averted her face, not wanting to see the expression in Blade's eyes as he looked down at the girl. No matter how carefully he might try to hide his true feelings, Kelly was afraid he might not be able to hide them altogether, and she wanted nothing to spoil this day, nothing to shatter the pretence that Blade loved *her*.

'We have to rush off,' Joe announced. 'We've a plane to catch. We're staying overnight in Sydney and flying home first thing in the morning.'

Kelly felt a wave of relief that they were going—that *Mary Lou* was going. She had thought that they might have been staying overnight in Melbourne as she and the Ryans were. A celebratory dinner at the Hilton, where Blade had earlier booked them in, had already been planned.

The remainder of that extraordinary Melbourne Cup day passed for Kelly in a dream-like trance, only partially induced by the champagne which flowed freely after Sherwin's phenomenal win. At dinner in the elegant Clivedon Room at the Hilton Hotel, Blade smiled at her as he raised his glass of champagne.

'I need one more thing to complete my happiness today.'

She became still, her heart giving a tiny jump. For a wild, sick moment she thought he was about to admit that he wanted Windarra Stud!

'How about setting our wedding date?' he asked.

It was so unexpected, she could only stare at him for a stunned moment.

'You mean—set the date *now*?' she said when she finally found her voice.

Something flickered across his face. Uncertainty? Wariness? And then it was gone, chased away by a quick smile.

'Yes, why not? I'd like to get married early in the New Year, things will be quieter then. A good time to take a long, leisurely honeymoon.' He sat back in his chair. The rest of the dinner-guests had fallen silent, hanging on every word. 'I imagine you'll want your family to come out for the wedding? So let's set the date now, then you can start making plans.'

He was watching her closely, as though trying to read her thoughts, the way she had been trying to read his a moment ago.

'Don't forget Dan and I are getting married in January,' Megan reminded him with her gentle smile.

Blade turned his head. 'What would you say to a double wedding?'

Megan's mouth dropped open. 'You mean it?' she cried, clapping her hands. 'Oh, that would be wonderful! But, Blade—you were going to give me away!'

'Ambler can give you away.' Blade glanced enquiringly at his brother.

'Be glad to. A double wedding sounds like a great idea,' Ambler agreed. 'Two separate weddings in the summer— in the same month—would be an intolerable strain on Mother.'

'On all of us,' Blade said with a grin. 'What do you say, Dan?'

'Suits me. Why not?'

Blade's eyes sought Kelly's, his hand closing over hers as it lay in her lap. 'What do you say, darling?'

She drew in a long, quivering breath, trying to hide the emotion that welled inside her at the endearment. It was the first time he had called her 'darling'. It was the first time, too, that he had brought up the subject of an actual wedding date. Did that mean he really was determined to go ahead with the wedding? Had she been wrong all along about Blade's feelings for Mary Lou, imagining they were deeper than was actually the case? Or had Blade, *despite* his feelings, made a cold, calculating decision to give Mary Lou up for good, because she, Kelly, offered more?

If only she weren't so blindly, helplessly in love with him, she might be able to think a bit straighter! She shook her head at the cruel irony of it. That she should have come to this! She, the girl who had always despised people who were at the mercy of their emotions, and now here it was, happening to her!

Blade's hand pressed her, and she looked up at him tentatively. His eyes were fastened to her face, and she saw something in the grey depths that made her catch her breath. Almost a yearning look.

She must be mistaken! Simple anxiety, more like, if he believed that Windarra Stud was at stake!

'Am I rushing you too much?' he asked gently, his expression masked now behind the hint of a smile and the flicker of his eyelids. 'Would you prefer to talk it over later, when we're alone?'

Alone! She felt his fingers stroking the back of her hand, awakening an immediate response, a tingling excitement, a longing to feel those same fingers sliding up her arms and over her body. How would she ever be able to think clearly once they were alone, once he held her in his arms?

'A double wedding sounds just fine,' she heard her voice answering, a voice that sounded strange to her own ears. Did it sound strange to Blade too?

A cheer went up around the table. She looked round, startled. She had forgotten for the moment that there were others present; others waiting for her reply too. Their faces were smiling; they all looked genuinely pleased. Turning back to face Blade, she saw that he was smiling too, the broadest, warmest smile she had ever seen, making him look younger, softer, and for the first time even vulnerable; making her want to take his head in her hands and tenderly stroke his face with her fingertips, exploring every crease, every bone, every hollow. She closed her ears to the treacherous little voice that tried to whisper that his smile was simply one of relief, not happiness; that he had what he wanted now.

CHAPTER TEN

GRACE RYAN's gentle face was wreathed in smiles when she welcomed them back to Bilba the next day. She had a special hug for Kelly, and words of comfort too, giving Kelly a warm feeling inside and an unexpected sense of belonging. It was as though Grace already thought of her as a daughter. She insisted that she stay for afternoon tea, and afterwards Blade drove her home. When they pulled up near the front steps of Windarra, he twisted round to face her.

'I won't stay now,' he said, resting his hand on her cheek as though he wished it could be otherwise. She wondered if he could possibly know what that tender touch was doing to her, and the sweet fantasies it aroused, the fantasy that he was beginning to genuinely care for her; that now that he had pledged himself to marry her, he was trying to forget Mary Lou and transfer his love to her.

Was that too much to hope for?

'Will you be back tonight?' she heard herself asking, the question popping out before she knew it was even in her mind.

She saw something flare in his eyes and felt a rush of warmth to her cheeks. Did he think she was inviting him to——

She dropped her eyes under his gaze. What *had* been in her mind? Seduction? Or a perfectly natural desire to see more of the man she had promised to marry?

Or . . . a little of both?

Blade's lips touched hers, and her eyes sprang wide, her heart fluttering, her lips ready to respond. But already he was drawing away.

'Not tonight,' he said regretfully. 'I've been away for two days; I have things to catch up on.'

She felt a ridiculous sense of disappointment, followed by a swift stab of unease. Was he planning to see Mary Lou?

She tried to ignore the pain that knifed through her at the thought. Wouldn't it be natural for him to want to see the girl, if he had been involved with her in the past? He would want to break the news to her about the wedding, to tell her it was definitely going ahead, and that they mustn't meet any more. . .

Blade wouldn't want to see Mary Lou again, would he, now that he was pledged to marry another woman?

Kelly realised then how much she had yet to learn about Blade Ryan—and how little time she had had to think through this greatest decision of her life. She hid a sigh. She had fallen in love with Blade Ryan against all reason, all logic, and she pitied herself for her lack of shame, her weakness. But some shred of her old self-confidence made her bury her shattered pride and be hopeful. He would grow to love her in time. She would *make* him love her! Already she knew he was not indifferent to her. She couldn't believe—refused to believe—that his kisses, his glances, his caresses meant nothing. It pained her beyond belief to think that they might be merely a means to an end, a way of getting his hands on Windarra Stud.

She became aware that Blade was watching her, his hands on her shoulders now, his fingers idly kneading the smooth silk of her jacket.

'You're very quiet,' he said, and she wished she could read the expression in his eyes. They had a disturbingly shuttered look. 'What are you thinking, I wonder? That you'll miss me, I hope?'

Alarmed that he might guess her true thoughts, she gave a careless laugh. 'I have work to catch up on too,' she said hastily. Lamely.

'I'll make up for it,' Blade promised, his hand giving her shoulder a squeeze. It was all she could do not to lean towards him and bury her face in his shoulder. 'I'll be over tomorrow to plan our engagement party—the guest-list and so forth. How does Saturday suit you?'

She looked up at him, her violet eyes appealing. 'We don't need a big party, do we, Blade? Just—just your family. *I* haven't anyone to ask.'

'Won't you want to invite your Windarra crowd?' he asked teasingly.

Her stomach swooped. That would mean inviting Mary Lou! Did Blade *want* Mary Lou to be there? Surely it would be too painful for both of them, for Mary Lou in particular.

There you go again, imagining there is something serious between them! She lifted her chin, a spark of her old spirit reasserting itself. Blade was marrying *her*, not Mary Lou. He had set the date for the wedding, and now he was anxious to plan their engagement party. Wasn't that all that mattered?

She smiled at him. 'Sure, I'll invite them,' she said. 'Naturally. I meant anyone *outside* Windarra.'

'We'll keep it exclusive,' Blade promised, smiling back at her, his fingers trailing across her throat, sending a shivery thrill down her spine as they slid round to lose themselves in the silky mass of her hair. 'God, it's tempting to stay . . . it's tempting to come back later tonight . . .'

She mustn't listen! She would only go weak again, and she had only just found some of her old strength and a glimmer of her lost pride. She was determined to hang on to both for as long as she could.

'No, you're right,' she said quickly. 'We have things to do. And—and I want to ring my mother and give her the news.'

'I hope she and Chuck will be able to come to the wedding,' Blade said, sounding as if he meant it. 'You don't expect them to be tied up with filming?'

'Mother's working on a telemovie at present, but shooting's due to finish early December. They did mention the possibility of coming out here for Christmas.'

'They still can—and stay until the wedding—it's only a week later.'

She could detect none of the old contempt in his voice, the contempt he had always shown for her mother. Was Blade Ryan mellowing? She looked at him half speculatively, half gratefully. 'It won't be easy for her—coming back,' she admitted. 'I'm glad you don't—don't——' she hesitated.

'Resent her coming?' Blade shook his head. His fingers

were still tangled in her hair, making it hard for her to concentrate on what he was saying. 'I think I understand better now why your mother left. Some people are suited to this life and others are not. It's as simple as that.' Quite an admission, for Blade Ryan! 'You, I believe, are,' he added, his eyes smiling now.

'Well, thank you,' she said, hiding the ridiculous surge of joy she felt. He was admitting at last that she belonged here! Was that part of the reason, she pondered hopefully, that he had asked her to marry him? She desperately wanted to believe that there had been more to his proposal than simply the need to save her reputation—Windarra Stud's reputation—or because he wanted Windarra for himself. She wished greedily that it could be more even than that, that he *felt* more. But it was enough, for now.

She woke late, haggard and heavy-eyed after a restless night tossing and turning, torturing herself with the thought that Blade might have gone to Mary Lou after all; imagining them together, speculating on what they would be saying to each other. Supposing Mary Lou managed to persuade Blade that he shouldn't go ahead with the wedding; that she, Mary Lou, his true love, must come first after all, even before Blade's coveted Windarra Stud? Would Mary Lou be strong enough, determined enough, to stand up to Blade and make him change his mind?

Before going to the stables as she usually did first thing in the morning, Kelly popped into the office to say good morning to Mary Lou. Was that her sole reason for popping in? she asked herself with a wry grimace; or was it to examine Mary Lou's face for tell-tale signs of the night before—of the truth?

She was surprised to find that Mary Lou hadn't arrived yet, although it was well after nine o'clock, her normal starting time. It was so unusual for the girl to be late for work that Kelly's fears came tumbling back. Where could she be? Had *she* slept in too? Kelly preferred not to dwell on the possible reasons why. Was she sick? Was she having trouble with her car? Had she decided it was too painful to come any more? Or was she with Blade?

Instead of going to the stables, Kelly sat down at the desk and tried to push her qualms aside by burying herself in the paperwork that had piled up in her absence.

But after a while she pushed the papers aside. She couldn't settle. Images of Blade and Mary Lou together kept popping on to the sheets of paper in front of her. She wished Blade would come. She needed desperately to see him again, to have him hold her and tell her again that he intended to marry her—that he *wanted* to marry her. In his arms she could convince herself that there was nothing between him and Mary Lou, or if there ever had been that it was over now, finished for good.

She heard the crunching of tyres on gravel. Blade already? Her heart gave a quick leap. Or was it Mary Lou? As she heard the car pull up outside, she pressed her face to the window. From where she was, she could just see the rear of Blade's familiar Land Rover in the shade of the big gum tree in the drive. As Blade's tall frame came into view, she heard another car, and saw Mary Lou's yellow Volkswagen come skidding to a halt alongside Blade's. Her heart plunged to her toes. Had their arrival at the same time been coincidental? Or had they driven here together? *Been* together earlier?

She saw Blade smile and wave as Mary Lou stepped from her car. Just as Kelly was about to turn away, she froze, unable to drag her eyes away from the scene that followed.

She saw Mary Lou run towards Blade. From this angle the girl's face was hidden from Kelly's view. As the two came together, Blade caught the girl in his arms and in the shadow of the spreading gum tree, wrapped her in a passionate embrace, his head bent over hers.

With a groan Kelly reeled away from the window. So it was true. No use fooling herself any longer. Blade still loved Mary Lou! He hadn't given her up—he had no intention of giving her up!

She gulped back the tears that rose chokingly in her throat. It was shatteringly clear. Blade would go on seeing Mary Lou, whether he married her, Kelly, or not. After all, he was only marrying her to get his hands on Windarra Stud! He had seen there was no point waiting around any longer for her to sell up and leave; he knew that if he wanted to possess Windarra, he would have to marry her.

But he clearly wasn't going to give up the woman he loved. Oh, no, Blade Ryan would want to have his cake and to eat it too!

What shall I do? She sank into a chair and buried her face in her hands. How could she go through with the marriage now, knowing Blade still cared for Mary Lou? How could she have considered such a mockery of a marriage to begin with? Had she lost all her pride, even to contemplate marrying a man who wanted only what he could get out of her? Even more humiliating, a man who was in love with another woman!

She sucked in her breath. She mustn't let them find her in here! They might guess that she had been watching them through the window, that she had witnessed that intimate little scene in the shade of the big gum. How could she bear to face them in any case, knowing what she knew now, having proof that her fears all along had been justified?

She grabbed a sheet of notepaper. The solution was suddenly perfectly clear to her. Painfully, agonisingly clear. She would give Blade what he wanted, right now, without him having to marry her first. He could have Windarra Stud—and his freedom! How could she go through with it now—marrying a man who didn't love her, when she loved *him* so much? She couldn't! And yet without him, she knew that she couldn't stay on in the valley. It would be too painful, to go on living so close to the Ryans, knowing Blade loved another woman, knowing he had only proposed to her, Kelly, because he wanted Windarra Stud. She might as well give him the place now, and let him live here with Mary Lou. At least she would know he was happy.

She started writing, scrawling the words in her haste.

You don't have to marry me, Blade. Marry the girl you love. You can have Windarra. It's what you want, isn't it? I'll leave as soon as the papers are drawn up. Will you arrange it all? Kelly.

There was no time for more, no time to dwell on what she had written, to refine the bald words. All she knew was that she couldn't face seeing either of them just now, that she had to get away for a while on her own. It would be less embarrassing for all three—and certainly less painful for *her*. Let Blade read the note first, let it sink in that she was giving him his freedom—giving him Windarra Stud— before they came face to face again for the painful handing over, and the even more painful leave-taking. The agony of leaving not only Blade, but the valley and the stud-farm she had come to love, was something she couldn't bear to think about right now.

She slipped out of the side door and ran like the wind.

'Saddle me a horse, will you?' she gasped when she saw Nico leading one of the stallions to his paddock for exercise. When she saw it was Redfern, she said quickly, 'I'll take Redfern. He likes to be ridden occasionally. Here. I'll hold him while you fetch his saddle.'

Nico looked at her doubtfully. 'Sure you can handle . . .' The question trailed off when he saw the look on her face. He handed Redfern over to her and disappeared into the tack-room.

Kelly tried to calm the big chestnut as he stepped backwards, tossing up his head.

'It's all right, boy. We're going for a ride. Steady, boy!'

She resisted the impulse to give Redfern his head straight away, riding him away from the stables at an intolerably sedate walk, warming him gradually first. Ahead she could see the shimmering green of the willows along the river bank, with the open paddocks beyond.

She felt numb. How could she bear to leave all this? But she mustn't think about it—not now. She must empty her mind and just ride. She needed time alone to gather her strength, to steel herself for the ordeal that lay ahead.

Smoothly, without loss of rhythm or tempo, the stallion's stride lengthened to a gallop. A wave of exhilaration swept over Kelly as the cool breeze streamed through her hair like fingers of silk, bringing a smile to her lips and a sparkle to her eyes. But the sparkle changed quickly to tears, tears that filled her eyes and momentarily blinded her.

And it was in that moment that disaster struck.

She never knew exactly how it happened. Blinded by her

tears, she failed to see the obstruction ahead, the log which lay in their path. If she had been prepared for it she would have jumped Redfern over the obstacle without any fuss, or steered him away so that he avoided the log altogether. But she was unaware of the danger ahead. Whether something—a bird, a rabbit—shot out from the log at the last moment to frighten Redfern, or whether he shied away of his own accord, she was never to know. It was only when she felt him baulk suddenly that she realised that anything was wrong—and by then it was too late. She was already catapulting over his head, her body striking the hard earth before she had time to react or protect herself.

After that everything went black.

She groaned softly, and heard a voice, as though in a dream.

'Kelly ... Kelly, my darling, are you all right?'

Gentle, comforting arms were holding her, cushioning her head and shoulders. Warm fingers were stroking her face, pushing her hair away from her brow. Her eyes fluttered open.

'Blade,' she whispered wonderingly. What was he doing here? Why wasn't he with Mary Lou? Why was he looking so worried?

She tried to rise and fell back against him with a moan.

'Where does it hurt?' Blade asked, his eyes shadowed with concern. Why *was* he so concerned? Why had he called her his 'darling'? Hadn't he read her note? Did he still think he had to keep up the pretence of being her loving fiancé?

'My shoulder,' she said, wincing as she tried to move again. 'I must have fallen on to my shoulder.'

'Better than directly on to your head,' Blade commented, looking relieved. 'You must have given your head only a glancing blow, thank God. Just enough to stun you for a minute or two.'

'I don't think it's dislocated or broken,' Kelly said, touching her shoulder gingerly. Blade was still holding her, she noticed, as though she were a precious, fragile object. 'Didn't you see my note?' she asked in a whisper.

She would have sworn she saw a look of genuine pain cross his face. 'Yes, I saw it,' he said, and his voice was rough with an emotion she couldn't read. 'That's why I came after you. You damn little fool!' he growled. 'What did you mean, Marry the girl I love? *You're* the girl I love. Do you think I'd want to marry you for any other reason?'

Now it was she whose face showed pain. 'Yes,' she said hoarsely. 'To get your hands on Windarra Stud. You always wanted it, you never pretended you didn't!'

He uttered an oath. 'I'll put that down to the blow on your head. I love *you*, you goose—Windarra's got nothing to do with it. I love you and admire you and respect you. I haven't looked at another woman since the day I met you. My foolish darling, do you think I'd ever let you go?'

She couldn't let him go on.

'Blade, I know about Mary Lou.'

His face went blank. 'You know *what* about Mary Lou? What's Mary Lou got to do with *us*?'

She looked away, unable to meet him in the eye, unable to bear his look of bemused innocence. She hadn't realised Blade was such an accomplished actor. Was he putting on this act merely to save her feelings? It was too late for that!

'Blade—I saw you kissing Mary Lou. I've suspected for some time that she and you——'

'*What?*' The word exploded from his lips, abruptly silencing her. 'You mean you——' He threw back his head in a sudden gust of laughter. 'My dear sweet imaginative darling, Mary Lou has just become engaged to Harry Watts! *That's* why I kissed her—I couldn't have been more delighted!'

'Mary Lou and . . . *Harry Watts*?' she echoed dazedly. 'But they—no!' She shook her head. 'I would have known.'

Blade kissed her lightly on the tip of her nose. 'Darling, you couldn't be expected to know. Mary Lou has kept her friendship with Harry a secret for weeks—she didn't want anyone to know about it until she was sure it was going to work out. After her break-up with Nico, you can understand her being a bit wary about saying anything too soon. I think I was the only one who knew—simply because I caught them together one lunch-hour, down by the river.

Mary Lou begged me not to tell a soul, and I gave her my word. In fact, since then I've even helped them once or twice to meet during working hours without arousing anyone's suspicions. Joe might have guessed, I suspect—but nobody else had an inkling. They've been models of discretion, you must agree.'

'You took Mary Lou out one evening,' Kelly protested faintly. 'I heard you call out to her that you'd "see her tonight" and that you were "looking forward to it". And next day she told me that someone had taken her out to dinner. Are you saying it wasn't you?'

'Not at all. I did take her out to dinner that night.' As her brow clouded in confusion, he explained gently, 'I took Harry out as well. It was Harry's birthday.'

Kelly's lips formed a soundless 'O'. Now she recalled Joe mentioning earlier that day that it was Harry's birthday and that he had given Harry the night of.

'Believe me?' Blade asked, looking down at her. He was laughing at her now. She could tell by the teasing light in his eye. She had made an utter fool of herself!

She nodded, asking stupidly, 'And they're engaged now?' He had already told her they were, but she needed confirmation.

'Dearest, if you had waited a few minutes longer you would have heard from Mary Lou's own lips. She was anxious to find you and give you the happy news. And compare engagement rings.'

Kelly involuntarily fingered the diamond on her left hand, the ring that in her haste she hadn't thought to leave behind with her note.

'I feel so ashamed,' she confessed. 'But——' she lifted her chin. 'I—I just wasn't sure about you, Blade. You—you never told me you loved me,' she accused.

A shadow passed across his face. 'You never told me you loved me either,' he pointed out quietly. 'All I knew was that I couldn't bear to think of my life without you. I was determined to have you. To marry you and *make* you love me. I knew you felt something for me, and that we had similar interests, similar ideals and ambitions. I knew that we belonged together. Living and working side by side. As *equals.* You've taught me, darling, that that's possible for a man and a woman, to live and work together as equals. My life without you now would be meaningless.' He brushed his hand across her brow with the tenderest of touches. 'So, I was sure I could make it work. If I didn't tell you how I felt about you, blame it on——' he paused, shrugging '—on stupid stiff-necked pride. I wanted to tell you, God knows, but the words wouldn't come,' he admitted. 'I was——' again he appeared hesitant, unusual for the decisive Blade Ryan '—afraid, I guess.'

'*You*, afraid?' When had Blade Ryan ever been afraid of anything? She almost smiled, but refrained when she saw that he was deadly serious now, his eyes gleaming like burnished pewter in the silver sunlight. 'Why?' she asked curiously.

'I don't know. Of having my feelings thrown back in my face perhaps, the way——' he stopped, his mouth tightening.

'The way my mother threw my father's love back in his face?' she asked softly. 'You knew how he had suffered over the years. Oh Blade, I had no idea. I thought—I thought——'

Her eyelashes fluttered downward, hiding her eyes. Again, she felt ashamed.

He put his hand under her chin and tilted it upwards. 'Look at me, Kelly. I don't blame you for thinking that way. At first Windarra *was* all I wanted. I never thought you would stay. You were an international show-jumper, used to the limelight, used to having lots of people around you. You had never lived in Australia before, let alone in an isolated spot like Windarra. And you looked so much like your mother that I imagined you must *be* like her too, and would come to miss your old life. When you proved you were different—and when I started caring for you in a way I didn't expect—I still wasn't sure you would stick it out. Why do you think I kept pointing out the obstacles, kept *testing* you? I had to be sure you had the backbone for this life, that this was what you really wanted, that it wasn't just a whim, a new challenge in your life that would pass. When you agreed to marry me, I thought it was only because you were anxious to save Windarra's reputation. You didn't say anything about loving me. In fact you—well, you seemed to be holding back.'

She laughed then, a soft gurgle of relieved laughter.

'I think we've both been suffering from the same malady—stubborn pride. I hid the way I felt about you because I didn't think you loved *me*. I—I thought Mary Lou was the one you loved.'

He shook his head at her. 'Do you honestly think a girl like Mary Lou would have been enough of a woman for me? She's a sweet girl, but I would have walked all over her. You will never let me do that to you, will you, my beautiful tormentor?' His hand sought hers and pressed it to his lips. Now he was smiling too, deep lines radiating from his eyes, transforming his face in a way that made her want to cry out with happiness at the tenderness she saw there. 'Darling, say it,' he begged. 'How *do* you feel about me? Forget your foolish pride and tell me.'

'Oh, I have no pride left now. None. I am completely stripped of all such pretensions. *You* have done that to me, Blade Ryan. No man has ever brought me to this . . . to my knees. I never thought——'

'Damn it, woman, I'll put you over my knee and spank you if you don't tell me what I want to hear.'

'Blade Ryan, you always were a domineering tyrant. *I love you*. There! Now are you satisfied?'

'Not quite. Say it again.'

'I love you. I love you and I never intend to let you go. Never! You're stuck with me!'

'Now,' Blade Ryan said, drawing her ever so gently into his arms, 'I am satisfied.'

With a radiant smile she reached up and curled her arms around his neck.

Miraculously, the pain in her shoulder had gone.

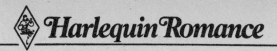
Coming Next Month

2941 WHIRLPOOL OF PASSION Emma Darcy
Ashley finds Cairo fascinating, and even more so the mysterious
sheikh she encounters in the casino. She's aware their attraction is
mutual, but doesn't take it seriously until he kidnaps her....

2942 THIS TIME ROUND Catherine George
It's all very well for Leo Seymour to want to share her life, Davina
thinks, but she can't forget that his first love married her brother
years ago. Would Davina's secret love for him be enough to sustain
their relationship?

2943 TO TAME A TYCOON Emma Goldrick
It isn't that Laura absolutely doesn't trust tycoon Robert Carlton;
she only wants to protect her young daughter from him. And Robert
has all his facts wrong about Laura. If there was only some way to
change their minds about each other.

2944 AT FIRST SIGHT Eva Rutland
From the time designer Cicely Roberts accidentally meets
psychiatrist-author Mark Dolan, her life is turned upside down.
Even problems she didn't know she had get straightened out—and
love comes to Cicely at last!

2945 CATCH A DREAM Celia Scott
Jess is used to rescuing her hapless cousin Kitty from trouble, but
confronting Andros Kalimantis in his lonely tower in Greece is the
toughest thing she's ever done. And Kitty hadn't warned her that
Andros is a millionaire....

2946 A NOT-SO-PERFECT MARRIAGE Edwina Shore
James's suspected unfaithfulness was the last straw. So Roz turned
to photography, left James to his business and made a successful
career on her own. So why should she even consider letting him
back into her life now?

Available in November wherever paperback books are sold,
or through Harlequin Reader Service:

In the U.S.
901 Fuhrmann Blvd.
P.O. Box 1397
Buffalo, N.Y. 14240-1397

In Canada
P.O. Box 603
Fort Erie, Ontario
L2A 5X3

Take 4 best-selling love stories FREE
Plus get a FREE surprise gift!

Taylor House

by Leigh Anne Williams

Enter the lives of the Taylor women of Greensdale, Massachusetts, a town where tradition and family mean so much. A story of family, home and love in a New England village.

Don't miss the Taylor House trilogy, starting next month in Harlequin American Romance with #265 *Katherine's Dream*, in October 1988, and followed by #269 *Lydia's Hope* and #273 *Clarissa's Wish* in November and December of 1988.

One house . . . two sisters . . . three generations

TYLRG-1